Room Of Echoes

Maya Hartwell (Quest for Justice)
Series Book 2

Gabby Black

ISBN: 9798395911117

Contents

Contents

Foreword

AUTHOR'S NOTE

Prepare to be captivated by the remarkable Maya, the protagonist of this series. Her backstory is as fascinating as her iron will and unyielding determination to uncover the truth, utilizing all the knowledge and skills she's accumulated throughout her life so far. Myself as a lover of suspenseful and thought-provoking entertainment media, particularly courtroom dramas, I've spent years refining my passion, and combining it with my background in the Justice System has led me to this moment. With a compelling narrative that keeps readers on the edge of their seats, the forthcoming books in the series will thrust Maya into increasingly intricate, nerve-racking, and suspenseful predicaments, both within and beyond the courtroom. Immerse yourself in a world that will thrill your senses and challenge your mind.

I warmly invite you to embark on this extraordinary journey alongside Maya and myself. I sincerely appreciate your time spent reading the second book in this 'Quest for Justice' series. Your interest and support hold immeasurable value, and I genuinely hope you relish the tale. To stay informed about

Maya's upcoming endeavors, kindly consider subscribing to my newsletter at **www.gabbyblack.com.**

Dear Reader

I would like to bring to your attention that this book in written in American English, which may differ in certain word choices and spellings from British English and Australian English. Throughout the narrative, you may encounter variations in vocabulary and expressions that are specific to American usage. I hope you find this linguistic distinction enriching, and that it enhances your reading experience. Thank you for joining me on this journey.

Warmest Regards
Gabby

Also By

BOOKS BY GABBY BLACK

Maya Hartwell (Quest for Justice) Series consists of;

Echoes of the Past Book One (Published on Amazon)
Room of Echoes Book Two (Published on Amazon)
Echoes of Betrayal Book Three (Published on Amazon)
Book 4 in the Quest for Justice Series Coming Q2 2024 or sooner!

Available in Audio

Echoes of the Past – available in US & UK
https://books2read.com/u/baq9O2
Room of Echoes – available in US & UK
https://books2read.com/u/m0WqvA

Prologue

Six years previously

Starting the ignition of my car, I can feel my stomach angrily growling at me, yelling at me to put something inside of it before it resorts to eating itself. It's been a long day, and I've spent the majority of my day in court. In that time I managed to forget to eat, and had to call off my weekly tee-time on the golf course. Before I took on this case, the courtroom was my happy place. However, I would've never thought I'd see the inside of it so much and so frequently. But really, what did I expect when I decided to take on the mob?

The Falcone Family is by far the most ruthless in California. The damage they have caused to the families of their victims ranges from San Francisco to Long Beach. Although I didn't have enough evidence to bring down the top "made" men of the family, like the boss himself, Frank Falcone or his consigliere and right-hand man, Henry Giancana, I was able to compile enough charges against his underbosses. Most of them consist of money laundering, tax evasion, and insurance fraud—but something is better than nothing.

To date, his case has been the most challenging one that I have ever had to prosecute. Not only have I had to keep the jury under 24-hour surveillance so they wouldn't be tampered with or bribed, but I, myself, have had Secret Service agents following me around since the men were arrested. It's been a major drain on both my mental health and my marriage. My wife doesn't feel comfortable sleeping in our home, and I can't say that I blame her.

Putting my car in gear, I start my long drive back to the countryside. Some days I really hate the journey it takes to get back to the comfort of my own home, but on days like today I find it quite relaxing. The weather isn't what I would consider perfect; long gone are the days of a warm ocean breeze as it has been replaced by freezing rain, and even the music playing on the radio isn't suitable for the day I've had. To top it all off, this is the weirdest weather I have ever seen, especially for California. *Mark one up for global warming, I guess.*

After nearly 45 minutes of driving on the expressway—slowly trying to make my way around the drivers who are going at a snail's pace—I turn left off the exit ramp and make a right onto a narrow country road. Almost immediately, I take notice of the large patches of ice that have taken over long stretches of the pavement and am forced to slow down to avoid skidding off into the grass. After sliding over one small patch and regaining traction, my eyes instinctively look into the rearview mirror to make sure the agents are still following closely behind but realize they are nowhere in sight. "That's strange," I murmur to myself.

With only a few miles to go until I can get home, have a nice meal and spend some precious time with my wife–if she recognizes me after all these long hours at the courthouse–I brush off any worries about the Secret Service taking the night off. From a distance, a vehicle with their high beams on is barreling toward me. Trying to avoid looking directly at the bright lights, I avert my eyes.

"Jesus, buddy. I know we are in the country, but the sun hasn't even set yet. There's no need for the high beams," I say out loud, as if the person can hear me.

The car comes further into view, their headlights blinding me with every quarter-mile they blow through. When the car is directly in front of me, the sound of exhaust booms as they hit the gas to go faster. *This guy really needs to slow down or he's gonna crash. Under these icy conditions there's going to be no way that he is going to be able to stop.*

Without warning, the car veers into my lane. Going too fast and giving me no time to react, the sound of crunching metal as the vehicle collides with mine amplifies throughout the car. My body is thrown forward with great magnitude, but is stopped by the interference of the airbag as it hits me square in the face.

The crumpling of metal and smashing glass seems to last for an eternity, but that could also be due to my car spinning around, only being pushed further as it hits another patch of ice. By the time my car comes to a complete stop, I'm feeling dazed and confused but can't be sure if it's due to the three full circles my car made after the accident or the blow to the face. My nose, which I'm almost certain is broken, makes it hard to breath and adds to the winded feeling the adrenaline rush has left me with. At least I was smart enough to put on my seat belt and I'll forever be grateful for the airbag absorbing the brunt of the impact, even if my face took most of the damage.

My consciousness begins to waver, and I'm fading out every couple seconds only to be brought back by the cool evening air being let in by the broken windows. From a distance, I can hear a car door opening and footsteps approaching. *They are*

*probably coming to check on me and make sure I'm still alive.
God bless 'em.*

Although my eyes are nearly swollen shut, I can vaguely
make out a hand coming in through the window to help me
out. "I'm so sorry about that, sir. I called the police, they are on
their way," the voice says in a strong accent. It's one I have never
heard before, making it hard to figure out where the driver may
be from.

Trying to put my hand up as a gesture of appreciation, I
quickly realize that my arm might be broken when I hear a loud
pop from my left shoulder. Slowly and painfully, I try to put my
hand inside his so he can help me out of my car. But by the time
it reaches him, his hand is no longer there. Trying to search for
his offering, I feel some slight tension on my neck.

The tension builds and tightens, and it hits me that the
pressure is caused by a hand around the back of my neck.
However, the skin of the palm doesn't feel normal. It feels
waxy, but smells like leather. *At least they are trying to help me,
and didn't just drive off like some asshole.* Trying to open my
eyes wider so I can see what's going on around me, a large dark
object gets closer to my face. I only realize the object is a gloved
hand when it is placed over my mouth and nose, and clamps
down on them. Shooting pain from my broken nose spreads
throughout the rest of my face, but I can't scream out. Letting
out a stifled moan, my body starts to feel adrift as darkness
comes over me.

·········

Coming to, confusion and panic sets in as I struggle for air. My
body is in survival mode and refuses to give in to the person's
barbaric demand for me to die. Trying to push away from him

with the small amount of strength I have in me, I am left feeling defeated. The strong grip on my neck limits my movements and leaves me unable to break free.

The unknown driver pushes his hand down harder, blocking off any air seeping in through the small cracks between his fingers. The lightheadedness takes over and I start to drift away from the real world again. The weight on my chest is lifted off me after the man pushes the release button of my seatbelt. The grip on the back of my neck gets tighter moments before my head is violently thrust forward into the steering wheel. A flash of light bursts in front of my eyes seconds before everything fades to black.

·······

Chapter 1

Present Day

As I get home from yet another busy day of work, I slowly transcend myself down onto my recliner and stretch my legs. Another win under my belt, my first win as a Senior Associate. Never in my wildest dreams did I think this day would come, especially after Blaine got promoted over me. However, all of his gloating and obnoxious tendencies seemed to float away when his dirty little secret was exposed. Imagine my surprise when everyone in the office discovered that he wasn't winning cases, he was paying people off! Everyone from the court clerk to the bailiff; sometimes even the witnesses taking the stand. I guess giving people a little incentive didn't make a big dent in his wallet when his client's payouts were in the six-figure range.

Needless to say, my bosses weren't very happy when they heard the news but I kinda was when I watched security escort him out the door with a box of his belongings in his hands. Mr. Richards called me into his office soon afterward, coercing me to take over Blaine's position, a definite edge in his voice suggesting it would be good for me and my career. Although I was overjoyed to become a Senior Associate, this wasn't really how I pictured earning the spot. I had always hoped that my work ethic, reputation, and ability to win cases would be what would do it for me, not someone taking the easy way out in order to beat the system. But the company needed to save face, and if anyone could do that, it was me. So, I accepted the job and have been busy ever since.

Taking off my heels, I rub my feet and curse the medieval torture devices. I still have no idea how some women can wear these things for fun. I'd rather wear combat boots for days on end than stand or walk for an hour in heels. Some days I feel like I look like a baby giraffe trying to walk for the first time, but then I remember that I have to appear confident in court so I focus on the task at hand.

Replacing the six-inch spikes for a pair of slippers, I make my way into the kitchen and grab the take-out containers filled with last night's leftover Chinese food out of the fridge. I dump the glutenous orange chicken onto a plate and pop it into the microwave, pushing the number two button so it can start cooking while I grab a fresh bottle of wine out of my pantry. This particular bottle was one I took from my father's large collection the last time I visited my mom. I've saved it for days like today, when I might feel the need to feel close to my father. It's a 2010 Rumpus Cellars Red from Sonoma County, a lovely Cabernet Shiraz blend. Goes very well with lamb, it says, *but that's subjective*, as my father would tell me. *We like what we like and with what we like!* That still makes me smile every time I visualize him saying it. Wine was one of his passions and he spent considerable time with me, telling stories of his visits to some of the biggest vineyards in the country and he got to know what's involved in the making of the delicious beverage.

Shoving a corkscrew into the top of the bottle, I give the simple machine a few turns and yank hard. A loud *pop* follows the uncorking, then the subtle pressure releases. The smell calls to me and I can't wait to pour a large glass, but I feel like something is missing.

It hits me what the missing element is and I run over to my couch to grab my phone out of my purse. With a few clicks of the screen, the phone links up to my bluetooth speakers and Pink Floyd begins to play. "Oh, Dad. I wish you were here to share a glass of wine with me and celebrate my first big win as a Senior Associate. I know you would be proud," I say out loud as I pour a healthy portion of the alcoholic beverage into a wine glass.

Almost as if my dad heard me, "Wish You Were Here" begins to play over the sound system. I sing along to the words and smile at the thoughts of my dad, imagining him standing next to me and giving me a toast. Before I realize it, the song is winding down but the last few notes are cut short when my text message notification sounds off through the room.

As I make my way to the phone, the microwave beeps and my stomach growls in response. Knowing texts don't require my immediate attention, I grab my plate and set it down on the kitchen table before checking my phone. Swiping up, I unlock the screen and see a notification that my friend Wren had texted me. It has been a while since we last saw one another in person, basically since he helped with the case on my last "vacation" in Landsfield Ridge. He's probably the most friendly librarian I've ever met. Had it not been for his impressive hacking skills, we may not have grown as close as we did. Our friendship has only gotten stronger since then, but the distance between us keeps all interactions at an electronic level. Double clicking the screen, I open the message and see the simple question.

Wren: Hey stranger! What have you been up to?

Unable to contain the smile caused by a message from an old friend, I begin to reply back to him. Mid-way through the message, the screen goes completely black before my ringtone starts to sing out. The caller ID takes a second to kick in and let me know whether to accept or deny the call, but finally remembers it has a job to do. When the face of one of my best friends from my time in the Marines is displayed on the screen, I let out a loud screech.

Under the name "Isabella," I press the bright green accept button to answer the phone and bring the device up to my ear. Trying to hold back my excitement to hear from her after so long, I greet her in the most normal sounding voice I can manage at the moment. "Hello?"

"Hey Maya! It's Izzy," she responds. Judging by the tone of her voice, I can tell the next few words out of her mouth aren't going to be good ones. Once I hear the words, "I–I need your help," I know I'm right.

Chapter 2

The phone buzzes against my ear, and I know it's probably another text message from Wren. But I choose to put my short conversation with him on the back burner as my gut tells me to place all of my attention on Izzy and whatever her problem may be. She has never called me and asked for my help before, so something must be very wrong.

Taking a sip from my wine glass, I clear my throat before responding. "What's going on, Izzy? Are you okay?"

"Not exactly, I guess. I don't really know to be honest with you. Some stuff has happened... like bad stuff... and I'm not sure what to do about it. I don't know who to talk to or who I can trust, really," she explains, her voice sounding defeated as if she has already given up.

Hearing her say that she doesn't know who she can trust makes me worry, almost more than the absence of happiness in her voice. Izzy is normally a very bubbly person and is always laughing or telling a joke, constantly drawing people in with her contagious laugh. But the person I'm talking to on the phone is void of any positivity, leaving me with a pit that seems to be taking over my stomach.

Clearing my throat again, I maneuver my mouth close enough to the receiver of the phone and clearly ask, "Are you somewhere safe where we can talk?" To the outside world it would be strange to ask her that question, but having been in the military, it's anything but. You never know who is listening in, spying on you, ready and willing to report your words to a superior officer. If she doesn't know who to trust, the last thing I want her to do is face more problems due to prying ears.

"Yeah, Maya. I'm good, for now anyway," she responds, her voice subtly quivering in hopes that I won't realize how scared she is.

When she doesn't start talking right away or beginning to explain, I push her along. "So what's going on? What do you need my help with?"

"I need an attorney–a good attorney who I can trust. Someone's out to get me and I need someone in my corner who will clear my name." Her voice cracks throughout her simple and direct explanation, and I can tell she's seconds away from breaking down on the phone.

Break down from what, though? Giving her a minute to collect herself and her thoughts, I finally ask her, "Who do you think is out to get you, Izzy?"

"The Marines," she responds, a loud gulp coming across loud and clear over the line. "I've been accused of murdering innocent civilians during my last tour in Afghanistan. I didn't do it though, Maya. I swear, I would never do something like that. As soon as the incident was reported, my commanding officer sent me home and I have been treated with complete hostility and been dismissed by everyone since I got here. Before you ask, no, I don't know why they would do this to me, but I do know that they are using me as a scapegoat to cover up what really happened."

"What did happen?" I ask, wanting to know what I may be getting myself into if I am actually able to help her somehow.

"I don't know that either. I didn't see anything, all I heard was guns shooting. But you know how it is on tour, you learn how to tune out gunfire because it happens so often. All I know is that I'm not willing to go to prison–military prison–for something I didn't do." My heart aches for her as she pleads her case to me, knowing that she is essentially up against a giant known as the United States government.

"I get it, Iz. Believe me, I get it." I pause for a second to think about what to say next. I don't want to get her hopes up but she's obviously depending on me. If I tell her that I can't do anything for her, considering I'm no longer a Marine, it would break her heart even more and I would feel terrible if she was actually punished for a crime she claims she didn't commit. "Um, have you been arrested or arraigned yet?"

"Not yet, but I'm sure that the court martial will be coming for me any time now. I just learned about the accusations made against me last night and you know how quickly they like to move these types of cases along." With every word, the stress in her voice grows stronger. If I were her, I would have skipped town already but being in the military, things run much differently than they do for civilians. The United States government would pull every punch, look under every rock and bridge, and toss the house of every person Izzy knows–especially if she is the center of a major cover up.

"Look, I don't want you to get your hopes up because I have to talk to my bosses about taking some time off. I'm in the middle of preparing for my next big case, but I am still going to do whatever I can to help you, whether I can get the time off or not. No matter what, I have your back so I don't want you to think you're alone in this, okay?" I remind her, hoping she hears what I'm saying. Even if the managing partners say I can't take a short vacation due to the upcoming court trial, I could at least find the best Judge Advocate General, or JAG lawyer near the San Diego base. If I am able to head that way, at least she's not all the way across the country; an eight hour drive at most if there isn't any traffic.

"I understand, but you are the only attorney I actually trust to get me out of this. Not this guy they assigned to take my case. Anyway, I can tell you the rest when and if you are able to come. There's too much to say over the phone," she hints, and I completely understand what she means. If the military is trying to cover up this murder then it's not safe to talk over the phone, as her phone could be tapped. The last thing she needs is for the Trial Council to find out her strategy and use it against her in court.

"Sounds like a plan. I will call you as soon as I find out if the visit is do-able. Take care of yourself, Iz." I hear her sigh in the distance and before she can hang up, I yell her name one more time. "Oh, and Iz?"

"Yeah?"

"Don't say a word to anyone until you hear from me, not even your lawyer!" I advise her.

"I won't. Thanks, Maya. Even if you can't come, I owe you one," she tells me graciously.

"No, you don't. You saved my ass enough when we were in the Marines, you will never owe me a thing. Why don't we just call it even?" I offer, hoping to make her feel a little bit better. However, with the situation that she's facing, it might take a little more than gratitude to get the job done.

"Deal. Bye, Maya."

The phone beeps, telling me the call has ended and I finally make my way back to the kitchen table, where my cold food awaits my presence so it can be eaten. Keeping my mind off the thick citrusy gelatin that has formed under my food, I try to figure out a way to bring up the idea of a quick leave to Mr. Richards. Luckily, Mr. Ryan is out of the country on vacation with his wife for their anniversary, so I only have to deal with half of the partnership instead of waiting on them to come to an agreement and give me an answer. Also, Mr. Richards is much more lenient than his counterpart in matters like this, so he might just grant me the leave I'm asking for if I explain what's going on.

No longer able to take another bite without keeping myself from gagging, I scrape the rest of my meal into the garbage and put my dish in the sink. As I rinse off the orange jelly from the porcelain plate, it hits me that I have been so wrapped up in Isabella's situation that I forgot to finish typing out my response to Wren. *He probably thinks that I'm ignoring him by now.*

I walk back over to the table and grab my phone, ready to finish what I was typing out to him, but decide at the last second to delete what I was going to write and start over. However, this time, I actually have something to send him rather than shooting the shit. As fast as my fingers can manage typing without making typos, I write him back.

Me: Hey Wren! I was just assigned a new case but I am unable to find any information as of yet. Do you think you could help me out?

Within seconds, he texts me back.

Wren: Sure. What's the defendant's name?

Me: Well, technically, she hasn't been arrested yet. However, she feels like it's only a matter of time. I just need whatever information I can get regarding the accusations against her. The name is Isabella Martinez-Garcia, she's a second lieutenant in the Marines.

Wren: And who is accusing her exactly?

Me: The United States Marine Corp. That's the catch, it might be a little difficult to find anything because some of the information may be classified.

I take a deep breath as I hit the send button and wait for him to respond. Hopefully, he could be of help in some way. Even if I am unable to get the okay from my bosses to take leave and visit her, I could at least see what Izzy is up against–possibly giving her a couple of pointers on what to tell whoever is assigned to defend her.

My phone rings, signaling that I have a new message. As I read Wren's response, I can't help but smile.

Wren: Ha! As if a little thing like classified information has ever slowed me down or stopped me before. I'll find what I can and overnight it to your house. Knowing the military, I'm sure all of the details in the reports could fill a binder so it would be easier to just send over physical copies.

Me: Thanks, Wren. You're the best!

Before I get the chance to set the phone back down and gather my bearings, he responds to my text in record time.

Wren: You always say that. But I'll get right on it! Now take some time to yourself and relax. Let me do the hard stuff.

Following his directions, I set my phone down and try to relax on the couch as I figure out what's on television tonight. I flip through the channels but don't find anything that calls out to me. Taking notice of the time, it's not even 9:00 p.m. yet, but I'm too mentally and emotionally exhausted to deal with any more bullshit today. Honestly, I'm not even in the mood to watch television for my last remaining hours of the night. Instead, I take a quick shower and jump into bed. Hopefully I'll be able to get some sleep and Wren will find something to send over so I can be of some use to Izzy.

Chapter 3

Waking up in the morning, I'm already feeling as if I'm in a trance of surrealness. It's almost as if I'm still stuck in my dreams, a nightmare that might never end. Maybe I am still dreaming, or maybe I'm just reeling from so much information being thrown at me at once. Izzy begging me for help really threw a curveball into my plans, and I wish for nothing else but to be able to help her. I don't even know why I feel like this, considering her accusations have nothing to do with me and I didn't feel this way last night. To make matters worse, the case preparation for my new trial has been hard, considering I'm fighting for the victims and former employees of a Forbes 500 company accused of criminally negligent conditions in their factories. Getting my witnesses to talk despite the NDA the company tried to impose on them has been hell on my normally average stress level, and I'm not sure if I can handle anything else being thrown at me at the moment.

Walking around the house in an effort to get ready for work, my feet feel like they are floating across the floor. *Am I experiencing that dissociation thing that I've heard so much about? Am I that close to being burned out or is my life just becoming too much for me to handle at once? Either way, I need to figure it out so I can put an end to it. I'm not going to be any good to my clients if I can't focus on their needs.*

Attempting to snap myself out of this terrible and negative mindset, I place all of my attention on what to wear for the day, making my morning coffee just how I like it, and ensuring that everything I need for my case prep is in my briefcase. Realizing I hadn't checked my phone when I first woke up, I run back to my room to yank my digital lifeline off of its charger. The screen turns on when the charging cord is removed from the port, but the only notifications showing up on the lock screen are spam emails, meaning Wren has yet to find anything or is still busy working on breaking through the Marine's barriers.

Once I'm finally ready to head to work, I lock my front door and jump in the car. Starting up the ignition, my brain goes on autopilot and pushes the CD button. As soon as Pink Floyd begins to ring through the speakers, I snap out of the distant state of mind and turn on the radio instead. At times like this—when I'm feeling stressed out—it only makes me miss my dad. Making me want to talk to him and ask him what I should do. Unfortunately, I'm unable to do that now and listening to his favorite album only reminds me that my mentor, guide, and best advice giver isn't here to help me out, which only makes me feel worse. Sadly, I forgot my auxiliary cord in the house so I can't turn on music through one of my streaming apps, leaving me with nothing except talk radio to listen to this morning. Talk radio has to be the worst thing to listen to, especially for people whose entire job is centered around listening to people's voices. Unfortunately, I don't really have a choice in the matter.

What usually feels like a quick trip to work, the deejay's droning voice makes my ride to the Ryan & Richards law office feel like a journey. By the time my car pulls into the parking lot, I start to feel how Frodo did when he finally reached the volcano in Mordor to throw that stupid ring in the damn volcano. *How am I supposed to get through the entire day when I already feel mentally drained? Today is going to be hell, I can already tell.*

Grabbing my briefcase from the backseat, I grab for my coffee cup in its usual holder but find that it's not there. I know for a fact I had it in my hand when I locked the front door, but only because it was difficult to juggle everything I had in my arms while trying to get the key in the lock. Retracing my steps, I try to remember what I did next. *I placed the cup on top of the car while I put my briefcase and files in the backseat, got in the car, and drove off. Oh, shit! I didn't grab it, did I?* Looking on top of my car, a wet coffee mark and the remaining residue reminds me that I should really pay better attention to what I'm doing. *Well, that's just great! Such an amazing way to start my day!*

Taking in a deep breath and pushing it out slowly, I shake off the bad mood that's trying to take me over, I ensure that I have everything I need for the day, and make my way toward the entrance doors of the building. Riding the elevator to the sixth floor, I take another deep breath before walking into the office and making the customary greetings to each employee at the front desk. "Good morning, Beth. Good morning, Judy." I say with the best smile I can manage at the moment, refusing to allow my own personal issues to get in the way of other people's mornings. It was hard enough to get the respect I deserve in my field, let alone the office itself, so the last thing I want is to put my coworkers on edge because I'm having a shitty morning. I hate attorneys like that; the ones willing to take out their anger on everyone they feel is beneath them; and I always swore to myself that if I ever became a Senior Partner I would never become one of them.

After putting my briefcase and small pile of case files on my desk, I grab my spare coffee cup that I keep in my bottom drawer, make the decision that it needs to be filled before I start working, and head down the hall to Mr. Richards' office. Just as I expected, he's sitting at his desk, reading over the morning paper. My newest case is bringing the firm a lot of media attention, which can be good and bad depending on what spin the journalist puts on it.

Looking over the edge of the paper, Mr. Richards spots me standing in his doorway and folds up the paper before placing it down on top of his desk. "Ms. Hartwell, good morning! How's your case discovery going? Getting all those damning witness statements in place?"

"Yes and no, sir. I still have a few former employees that haven't answered my voicemails but I plan on following up with them today. I need to talk to you about something, and it's kind of personal." I cringe at saying the issue is personal, because while it has to do with my private life, it's not really my issue.

Nodding his head, Mr. Richards gestures toward the chair, welcoming me in. Closing the door behind me, I sit in the seat across from my boss and pensively place my hands in my lap so I can fight the urge to fidget. Starting off the conversation, Mr. Richards opens up the floor. "So, what do you need to speak to me about, Maya?"

Fighting back the urge to sound like I lack confidence, I bite my tongue before I start explaining my predicament with "um." Maintaining eye contact and perfect posture, I begin, "I may have overstated the importance of the discussion. However, the subject is very important to me. One of my friends from my time in the Marines called me yesterday and told me she was being accused of murder during her time on tour. I need to head down to the San Diego Marine Base and see if I can help her in any way. If you allow me to take a quick leave, I can be back in two days—three at most."

Clearly trying to digest all the information I fed him, Mr. Richards sits quietly in his chair and rubs his chin, his tell that he's considering what he has heard. Giving him the time to think over what I said, I sit quietly in the chair and continue to fight the need to pick at my nails or twiddle my thumbs. After five minutes, he finishes thinking it over and leans forward to give me his decision, "Maya, I understand the situation and although I sympathize with your friend's circumstances, I can't afford to allow you to leave on another vacation. This negligence case is the biggest trial we have ever had on the books, so your leaving gives you less of a chance to bring justice to the victims who need it."

Although I can feel my temper flaring at what my boss is saying, I push it deep down and keep my composure as I plead my case. "With all due respect, Mr. Richards, I'm fairly certain I can handle prep work while I am away. The trial doesn't begin for another couple of months, and I am already way ahead of schedule. Not to mention, I have single-handedly saved this company from financial ruin as well as humiliation in the press after the whole Blaine incident. So, please, would you try to reconsider your decision?"

Mr. Richards bites his lip, obviously taken aback by the counterargument I just gave him. He definitely didn't expect me to respond in that manner, but I feel like I had no other choice. Patiently waiting as he tries to figure out what to do, I give him a small smile. With a tiny nod and a rub of his white mustache, he responds, "I'll think it over and give you an answer by the end of the day."

Standing up from the chair, I put my hand out to shake his. Mr. Richards stands up as well and takes me up on my offer, but it's obvious that he's reluctant about doing so, giving himself away with a lackluster grip. "Thank you, sir. I really appreciate it."

"If I decide to give you this leave, you better not let me or this firm down. You may be one of the best Senior Partners in the office, but you aren't irreplaceable. Even though you will technically be 'on leave,' this case, should it move any further, is to be an independent project. As you know, we don't defend clients accused of murder, so our firm is not to be associated with this case in any way. Now, please go. I have a meeting I have to get to and you have follow up calls to make," Mr. Richards commands, his voice strong and firm.

"Yes, sir. I completely understand. Thank you," I tell him one last time before walking through the same way I entered and closing the door behind me so he can have some privacy. When I arrive back at my desk, I pull the list of phone numbers of witnesses who require a follow up call, pick up my phone, and get back to work.

After five successful connections and leaving three voice-mails, I place the phone down and open my laptop to get some motions typed up for the case. Before I know it, lunch time has arrived and I'm ready to stuff my face. Although I prefer to leave the office to eat lunch, I decide against it and place an order with a local deli to be delivered. For some reason, I had the strange feeling that if I were to leave my desk, I might miss Mr. Richards' decision and he could change his mind.

My order of turkey and provolone on rye with a bag of salted kettle chips and a Diet Coke, sans the ice, make for the perfect lunch to eat at my desk. No mess, except for the juice from the pickle slice, and extremely filling for being so light. Wiping the small amount of crumbs off my hands and into the trash can—along with the food wrappers—I get back to work as I start drafting subpoenas for the victims I haven't been able to get ahold of. I hate sending out subpoenas, but if no one calls me back then I will be forced to send them. Really, it's more of a formality to have them typed up and ready to go in case they are needed. This busy work also gives me something to do while I wait on Mr. Richards to give me his final decision on the whole short leave situation.

Four o'clock finally comes and goes, and I have yet to see my boss. He normally leaves at four-thirty, so I am really hoping that he doesn't try to dip out of here without giving me an answer. Izzy is waiting on my call, and my patience is starting to run out. As I finish up my last subpoena, a man passing by my office catches my eye and I lift my head to see who it is. When the person doesn't back up and poke their head in, I realize it wasn't him. As I wait in excruciating agony, my thoughts begin to wander, questioning whether I was out of line with how I spoke with my boss earlier. *No, I wasn't. I was open, honest, and assertive with him, just like Dad taught me to be. I made my needs known and didn't allow his threat to replace me throw me off my game. If Dad had seen me in action, I know he would've been proud.*

Keeping myself busy all day makes it easier to focus my attention off everything going on with Izzy and I just wish I could pick up the phone so I could give him a call. He always gave me the best advice, but now as I sit here on pins and needles, waiting for Mr. Richards, I feel stuck in my head as I wonder what I could possibly do for her from here if I am unable to leave.

My clock hits 4:35 p.m., and still no sign of my boss. He had to have taken the other door so he could avoid passing by my office, giving me his decision non-verbally and with extreme cowardice. "What an asshole," I murmur to myself.

"I'm sorry. Are you on the phone?" a voice coming from the doorways asks.

Closing my eyes for a brief second, I look up from my desk and see Mr. Richards standing outside my office door, briefcase in hand and ready to head home for the night. Shutting my laptop, I attempt to explain, "Oh, no. Sorry, my laptop died while I was mid-sentence."

Completely disregarding what I had said, Mr. Richards gets down to business. "Anyway, I thought it over and have made a decision. Seeing as I'm a former military man myself, and you have the opportunity to help to save the life of a fellow Marine, I feel like it's only right to allow you to take a few days off to see if you can be of service to your friend."

Standing up from my chair out of respect, I place my hands behind my back and smile at Mr. Richards gratefully. "Thank you so much, sir."

"No need to thank me, just make sure you hold up your end of the bargain. You can't fall behind on your case preparation and must be back in a few days. Again, I can't help but stress the importance of this case," he reminds me.

"I completely understand, Mr. Richards. I will notify all of my clients that they can contact me on my cell phone and have the receptionists direct any of my incoming calls to my cell as well," I inform him, trying to hide how happy I am and maintaining my professionalism.

"Very well. Have a safe trip, and I will see you in a few days." Without allowing me to respond, Mr. Richards turns around and walks away.

Overjoyed—yet feeling a little indifferent on the reason for the visit—I pull my phone out of my desk and call Izzy. When she doesn't answer on the fifth ring, the call goes to voicemail. *Hm, she must be busy or maybe she's meeting with her lawyer.* After the beep, I leave her a short message. "Hey, Iz. Just wanted to let you know that I got the thumbs up from my boss so I will be heading your way first thing in the morning. I should be there around one or so, depending on traffic of course. I'll call when I'm close. Bye."

Ending the call, I open my text inbox. Although I'm aware that I don't have notifications of a text from Wren, I check just in case my phone forgot to notify me. Weirder things have happened, right? Technology can't be perfect all the time. Unfortunately, there aren't any texts waiting for me from Wren, or anybody for that matter.

Although he hasn't found any answers yet, I feel the need to let him know I'll be in San Diego for the next few days but will have my phone on me at all times. Hitting the little button with the paper airplane symbol on it I send Wren the text, put my phone in my briefcase, and collect my things. But before I can get anything put into my bag, my phone buzzes and I find a message from Wren, stating that a package has been delivered to my front door.

I shoot back a quick text, thanking him again and reminding him how amazing he is before I finish grabbing my things. I find myself skipping to my car on my way out of the office, strangely excited to get home and pack my clothes so I can head to San Diego to see my best friend. It might not be the best circumstances, but at least I can be there to support her.

Chapter 4

After a long drive, the eight hours I planned plus the two I was forced to sit in traffic for after a semi crashed into a Ford Bronco, I'm more than ready to stretch and hang out with Izzy. As I pull into her driveway, I see her car parked and my body is buzzing with excitement. I haven't seen her in so long, and although this isn't the ideal situation for a visit, I miss her. She became my best friend right after we met, and it's a shame we didn't make time to see each other more often after I was honorably discharged and she decided to stay in the service. However, we both have busy lives, and responsibilities have a tendency to get in the way of adult friendships.

Putting my car in park and shutting off the ignition, I exit my car and stretch my legs, shaking out the soreness I'm holding deep in my muscles. Feeling too excited to grab my bag from the trunk, I decide to run up onto the porch and ring the doorbell. I wait there for a few minutes, but no one answers. She has never had a roommate because she doesn't like living in shared spaces. I totally understand her need to have time alone, especially after staying in such close quarters in the barracks. Unfortunately, her not having a roommate screws me because there's no one here to answer the damn door or wake her up if she's sleeping in.

I had tried to text Izzy a few times while I was stuck in traffic to let her know I'd be later than planned. Then, I called her at least four times when I finally started moving, and twice when I was close. All of my calls and texts went unanswered, which is totally unlike her. The alarm bells were ringing in my head the whole trip, but I tried to keep calm until I arrived—just in case she had gone out for a run or forgot to charge her phone. Anything is possible. *Anything...* Now that I'm here, she's still not answering the phone. In my gut, I can feel something is wrong, but I don't want to jump to conclusions. The Marines wouldn't go through the effort of a court marshall if they were just going to do away with her! *God I hope she's alive. Her car's here so I assume she would be here, too. Something isn't adding up, though. What happened to her? Where could she be?* I knock a few more times, but there's still no answer and I start to panic.

Rather than standing on the porch like a jackass or door-to-door salesman, I step off the porch and take a peek in the windows as I move toward the back door. It's kind of eerie to see no movement in the house; no lights on in any of the rooms on the first floor; no television on. All I can see is a full plate of food on the kitchen table and a cup of coffee knocked over, the dark brew leaving a large, dried splatter onto the hardwood floor. My eyes move onto the countertop where pans are on the stove and a load of dishes are sitting in the sink. The disorder of her kitchen sends up red flags in my head because Izzy is one of the cleanest people I know. She freaks out if a spoon or cup is in the sink, and a full sink would send her obsessive-compulsiveness into overload.

Once I reach the fence that separates the side of the house from the backyard, I unlatch the lock and climb up the small set of steps attached to the back porch. Cupping my hands around my eyes, I look through the glass of the sliding door to see if I'm missing anything. My heart pumps harder and faster with every strange feature of the room; items in disarray around the normally clean house that tells me something happened here. I can tell by the untouched breakfast on the kitchen table that whatever occurred was hours ago, as I know Izzy likes to be up and walking around before the Sun even shows its face. My stomach drops when I notice what looks like drops of blood on the floor around the island in the middle of the kitchen.

"Excuse me! Can I help you?" a husky voice calls out from behind me, scaring me enough to make my racing heart nearly skip a beat.

Spinning around toward the sound, the wind is knocked out of me when I see a large man in a bright white T-shirt and dark cargo shorts standing on the porch of the neighboring house. Realizing how this looks from his perspective, it hits me that a stranger looking into his neighbor's home might be considered a little suspicious. My eyes flash down to the logo on his white shirt for a split second and notice the word "Wounded Warriors Battalion-West" across his chest. Putting two and two together, and remembering I'm on a military base, I use this to my advantage.

"Hey, my name's Maya Hartwell. I'm looking for my friend, Isabella. We used to be in the Marines together." I explain, earning a nod from him as the somber look on his face disappears. Whether you are currently in the military or a veteran, Marines always show one another respect, so sharing with him that I was once a serviceman removed any suspicion on his part. Once his scowl has disappeared from his face, I continue with my explanation regarding my strange behavior. "She's supposed to be here but she's not answering the door, and her car is in the driveway. I know you probably don't make it a habit to spy on your neighbors, but do you have any idea where she might be? She's not answering her phone and I'm starting to get worried."

The man shrugs his shoulders, keeping his stone-faced expression as he speaks, "You're right, I don't make it a habit to know what everyone is doing. But it was kinda hard to ignore the chaos going on this morning, it disrupted my morning workout."

Furrowing my brow, a wave of confusion washes over me. "What are you talking about? What happened?"

"She got swatted. A whole SRT–the, um, Special Reaction Team–kicked in her door at six a.m., yanked her out in her pajamas. I've never seen a fellow Marine get removed from their house before, especially twenty something officers for a petite girl like Izzy. She's a nice, quiet girl so whatever she did must've been fucked up." Without another word, the man turns around and walks back inside his house.

Standing on her back porch, frozen in shock, the news transforms my confusion into anxiety. *Izzy has already been arrested? Yanked out of her house no less, by the Special Reaction Team in her pajamas?* Walking back around to the front of the house, I approach her front door and take a closer look at the white frame bordering the entryway. The splintered wood surrounding the knob is proof that her door was kicked in, and I'm in disbelief that I somehow managed to miss it when I first arrived. Then again, I was too excited to see my best friend to evaluate the state of the doorway.

I have to do something. I need to see her and find out what's going on. Checking the time on my phone, the screen flashes 5:00 p.m. Isabella was taken into custody almost 11 hours ago, so by now she's most likely been booked and given a prison cell. Realizing I no longer have a place to stay, I rush downtown to find anywhere with a vacant room.

Luckily, I find a decent hotel and quickly check in, drop off my bags, and head toward the brig just outside the Marine base. As I drive up to the iron gate, I come to a stop at the officer standing guard and hand him my driver's license and veteran identification card. He takes a quick glance at the cards, hands them back to me, and pushes the button to open the gates. As I prepare to drive through the opening, the prison guard gives me a salute and thanks me for my service.

Returning the salute, I drive into the parking lot and find an open spot next to the entrance doors. The moment I exit my vehicle, a flood of memories hit me all at once. Between the high pitched screech of the Sargeant's whistle in the distance—presumably being used to torture the new cadets during drills—and the smell of expelled gunpowder from the nearby practice shooting range, I feel as if it had only been a few days since I last stepped foot on base rather than years. Keeping both identification cards and my cell phone in my hand, I throw my purse in the trunk so I can make the search process easier and get to Izzy sooner. Repeating the same process with the scowling older woman at the front desk, I hand her both forms of identification.

In a scratchy voice, one you would expect from someone who has smoked cartons of cigarettes for the past 40 years, she asks, "Who are you here to see?"

"Second Lieutenant Isabella Martinez-Garcia. I was told she was picked up this morning by SRT, and I need to speak with her." The woman pursed her lips at the mention of Izzy's name and I can only assume she knows the accusations against my dear friend.

"May I ask your relationship to the prisoner?" she asks, sending my head into a tailspin with the use of the word *prisoner.* I never thought I would hear that word and attribute it to Izzy.

She's not a prisoner, she's a soldier. Growing impatient by the amount of time I've stood in front of her and have yet to answer her question, the officer rudely derails my train of thought and snaps her fingers in front of my dazed face.

"Ma'am, I need to know your relationship to the prisoner. Her paperwork hasn't come through yet so I don't have the ability to see who she is allowed to accept visits from."

Snapping out of it and putting my attorney hat on, I stand up straight and look the woman directly in the eye. "She called me yesterday when she learned of the accusations against her. She asked me to represent her if an arrest were to occur. So, to answer your question, I'm the prisoner's lawyer."

"Alright. I will inform the guards that you are here and will call your name when she has been placed in the room we designate for attorneys and their clients. Please have a seat," she states calmly, although the look in her eyes doesn't match her words. They are sending daggers through me, piercing my skin, and I can only imagine the thoughts going through her head. I may not be a JAG attorney, but it's not like I'm just some ambulance chaser Izzy yanked off the streets. I was a Marine at one point in my life and was honorably discharged, so her attitude toward me is completely unnecessary.

Sitting patiently in a plastic and dull gray chair in the corner of the waiting room, I wait for my name to be called. Minutes tick by before I pull my cell phone out and check my email, only to hear the guard at the front desk clear her throat and point out the sign stating cell phone use is prohibited in the building. Putting up my hand to signal my apology, I slide my phone back into my pocket and watch as people who arrived after me get called back to the visiting area. Fifteen minutes slowly turn into forty-five, and before I know it, a full two hours have come and gone. *This is bullshit!*

I get up from my chair to speak with the woman at the front desk, only to find a new guard sitting in her place. Her replacement is a much more pleasant officer, and he greets me with a big smile. "Hello, ma'am. May I see your identification and get the name of the prisoner you are visiting?"

"I've been waiting for two hours to be called back so I can meet with my client, Second Lieutenant Isabella Martinez-Garcia. The woman who was here before you was supposed to let the guards know so I could speak with her in the attorney's meeting room," I explain, trying to keep the tone of annoyance out of my voice. My wait has nothing to do with the new guard, so it's not right for me to take my anger out on him.

He gives me a look of concern, and holds up a finger as he begins to type on his computer. "I apologize for your wait, miss. Let me check this out for you real quick." Pressing the button on the side of his radio, a static noise sounds off before he starts speaking. "Does anyone have eyes on Inmate 57482441? Her attorney has been waiting here for three hours to speak with her," he announces, winking at me when he exaggerates how long I've been sitting in the waiting room.

A second later, the voice of another guard speaks over the radio. "First time hearing she had an attorney waiting to see her. Inmate's just finished eating their meal in the chow hall. Taking her to the meeting room now."

A different guard—a muscular man with a shaved head—moves to the inside of the door and waits for the helpful officer at the reception desk to unlock the barricade between the waiting room and the prisoners. A loud buzz rings through, followed by a click, and a guard on the other side of the entryway turns the knob and opens the heavy door before nodding in my direction. As I pass by the front desk, I give the officer a gracious smile, although I'm cursing the woman who previously sat in his chair for wasting two hours of my time.

The guard escorts me to a small room with a thick perspex screen and points at the stool where I'm supposed to sit down. After a few minutes, Izzy is brought into the room by two marines and ordered to sit on the other side of the screen. She is dressed in shorts and a baggy sweatshirt, which I can only assume is either the prison uniform or what she was wearing when she was arrested this morning. One of the guards pulls out a ring of keys and searches for one to unlock the cuffs holding her hands behind her back while the other bends down to attach the leg irons to the bottom of the table. Izzy hangs her head, staring down at the floor in a combination of shock, disbelief, and shame, and I stand up from my chair.

With an undertone of disgust in my voice, I address one of the guards before he gets a chance to unlock the cuffs, "Why is she being treated like this?"

The guard stops looking for the handcuff keys and looks past me as he responds, "Suicide watch, ma'am."

"This is ridiculous. My client is not suicidal, nor has she ever been in all the years I have known her! I want these off now!" I command, pointing at the leg irons. "Not a single cuff either. You tell your CO that we want all these off or I will be filing complaints with all members of the Senate Armed Services Committee. Your CO will go blind with paperwork."

"Yes, ma'am," the guard states, still refusing to look directly at me. Snapping his fingers at Izzy, he yells at her to stand up and is about to grab her arm forcefully to lead her out of the room but stops when he sees the look on my face. As she is led out of the room, I sit back down and get comfortable while I wait for her return, hoping that their reluctance to follow my orders doesn't lead me to sit here for another two hours.

Izzy returns to the room 10 minutes later, this time dressed in fatigues and without cuffs or leg irons locked onto her person. Once again, she looks down at the ground while she takes a seat and only looks up at me when the guards leave the room.

Normally, guards are required to stand in the room during regular prison visits; however, since I signed in as Izzy's legal representation, they have to stand outside the room so we can have some privacy. Staring into the eyes of the woman across from me, the empty void behind them causes me to worry. Her face tells me that she's silently freaking out over what to do, but her demeanor displays nothing short of complete and utter numbness. It's clear that she knew this day was coming, but the reality of the situation has caused her to mentally, emotionally, and physically shut down.

Giving her a comforting smile, I decide it's best to start off our conversation. "I had my friend dig up whatever they could on your case and receive your charge sheet. They are accusing you of Article 12, conduct unbecoming; Article 90, disobeying a senior officer, Article 22, assaulting a senior officer; and Article 118, murder in the first degree. What happened?"

Without moving her head, Izzy looks around the room before responding in a defeated and low voice, "Like I told you on the phone, I'm being set up. They just want to pin this all on me."

On the off chance that I can take on her case—the fact that I am no longer in the military, and most of the evidence may be considered confidential—I ask her for more details, "What happened? I need you to tell me everything you remember the day of the shooting."

Izzy nods her head that she understands, and I watch her face transform from a feeling of numbness to one of remembrance.

"We arrived on the outskirts of the village. The commander asked me to get out and watch the road. If any Taliban or hostiles turned up, I was supposed to radio it in and he ordered me not to leave my post until they returned. Fifteen minutes later, I heard gun fire from the village. I radioed to see what the commander wanted me to do. He told me that they had a situation, but I was to hold my post. Ten minutes later, they came out. Two of the squad exited the vehicle, took my gun off me, threw me to the ground, and put cuffs on me. I kept asking what's happening and they told me I was under arrest. That's all I know."

Running her fingers through her greasy and matted hair—a sign that she didn't have a chance to run a brush through it before the SRT team kicked in her door—her face only grows more weary with every detail of the story.

Trying to maintain my objective from the attorney's side, I push my feelings for my friend aside. Although I wish more than anything that I could comfort her, I can't help her if I allow my emotions to cloud my judgment. Clearing my throat, I ask her a follow-up question. "So they didn't tell you why you were under arrest when they tackled you?" Izzy shakes her head in response, leading me to my next question. "How did you find out about the accusations made against you, then?"

"My commander told me right before they put me on a plane and sent me back to base. I called you as soon as I got home because I knew that if you were able to help me, it may take a couple of days for you to get your affairs in order. I was just hoping that you would be able to get here before I was arrested." Moving her eyes around the room and blinking rapidly, I can see that she's trying her best to fight back tears. Suddenly, a flash of anger explodes across her face and she lashes out unexpectedly. "Do you know what they are going to do to me, Maya? They're going to put on a court martial. A kangaroo court. They'll probably do it behind closed doors so that it's guaranteed that they will find me guilty, and then they'll lock me away in some god awful place, or maybe some special Pentagon facility no one's ever heard of, for the rest of my life. Which I can only assume won't be long, because soon they'll 'discover' me dead in my cell–presumably a suicide."

Taken aback by her outburst, I attempt to fight back my own tears. Looking down at her hand on the table, I feel the urge to hold it but the glass screen between us makes it impossible. Rather than using physical touch to comfort my friend, I go another route and use my most calming voice when I speak with her. "Holy hell, Izzy. We really need to find you an attorney."

Shaking off her tears, Izzy furrows her brows and cocks her head to the side. "You can't defend me? I thought that's why you came."

"Izzy, what the hell do I know about military justice and court procedure? I'm not a defense attorney, I fight for victims of big corporations," I explain, hoping she will understand. "As much as I want to help you, I'm not sure if I'm the best man for the job–so to speak."

"Then you should speak with the allocated military attorney they assigned to my case. His name is Tom Braseford. He's not only a lawyer but he's a First Lieutenant so he'll know all the military stuff and can teach it to you. You're a fast learner and should be able to pick it up in no time." Her pupils grow large in size, nearly taking over every millimeter of her brown irises, as she pleads with me.

Wanting to make my position on the subject clear while proving that I am here to help her, I ignore her pleas and make my voice more firm. "I have a big case coming up, Izzy, and I have people who are depending on me at work. I came here to help you any way I can, but I'm not sure if I can do what you're asking me. These cases can take months, and I don't have that kind of time. We have to find you an outside attorney who really knows what he's doing, in addition to the one they assigned to you."

Izzy sits frozen in her chair as her once almost hopeful expression returns to the lost and numb appearance she had when she first entered the room. Her mouth begins to move, but no words come out. I really need her to say something, anything, so I know she understands what I'm trying to tell her. Her eyes fixate on mine a few minutes later and she opens her mouth to speak but is interrupted when the guard enters the room.

"Time," he announces.

"We're not finished yet," I tell him. "You don't have the right to cut short any correspondence between an attorney and a client."

"Sorry," the guard responds, shrugging his shoulders before he wraps his large hand around Izzy's forearm and helps her up from her stool. "Commander's orders."

Still standing there, I feel the rage I felt in the waiting room slowly return and begin to amplify when the sound of the metal door closing echoes off the walls of the painted brick room. A guard taps me on the shoulder, bringing me back to reality, and signals with his head to follow his lead. I follow the guard back into the search area, endure the quick pat down, and am escorted back into the waiting room.

As I walk past the front desk on my way out, the officer who refused to help me and made sure I was stuck waiting for hours on end gives me a smirk and tells me to have a nice day. *Bitch*! Shoving the door open, I take a deep breath of fresh air and pull my phone out of my pocket. Tapping on the screen, I notice a text from Wren, making sure I was satisfied with the information he had sent me.

I open the text and send a quick response back to him.

Me: Yes, thank you. But I'll call you later tonight when I get back to my hotel room. I have to meet with a potential client.

Within minutes, Wren sends me a text back.

Wren: Good luck!

Thanks, Wren. I'm gonna need all the luck I can get.

Chapter 5

After sending a text over to Wren, I type the name of Izzy's assigned defense attorney into my Internet browser and hit the search button. Seeing that his office is only a couple of streets away is a godsend because this is my first time in San Diego and I have no idea where I'm going. I've been basically relying on the maps app on my phone to get where I need to go the entire time.

Pulling into the small parking lot beside a tiny office that had obviously been a home at some point, I turn off my car and walk onto the porch. Double checking the address first, I match the numbers with my Internet search and knock on the door. A mountain of a man with salt-and-pepper hair, crystal blue eyes, and pythons for arms answers the door, his voice gruff and deep as he greets me. "May I help you?"

"Hi. Are you First Lieutenant Tom Braseford by chance?" I ask, looking up at the man who towers over me by at least a foot and a half.

The man cocks his head to the side, raising one eyebrow, as he crosses his arms over his chest. "I am. And who might you be?"

Normally I don't find myself feeling nervous or intimidated by other people, but the energy Tom exudes stifles me for some reason. Whether it's his size or just his overall take-no-shit demeanor, I'm feeling myself a little lost for words. "I'm—um—My name is Maya Hartwell. I'm friends with one of your clients, Isabella Martinez-Garcia. She asked me to speak with you about her case."

"Oh, okay. You're the friend she was telling me about. The ex-Marine turned attorney, right?" he asks, his expression softening a little bit. Stepping to the side, he allows me to enter his office and offers me a seat.

"Yes, sir." I respond, allowing myself to take a load off in his comfortable chair. Between the seats in my car, the hours in traffic, the stool in the visiting area, and then sitting on those uncomfortable plastic nuisances they call chairs in the prison, my lower back is killing me and his cushiony lounge chair is an answer to my prayers.

Tom moves over to the coffee pot and pours himself a cup before looking over and pointing to his cup, asking me if I would like some. Shaking my head, he takes a seat at his desk and takes a sip before continuing on with our conversation. "So, you want to talk about your friend's case, huh? What about the case caught your interest?"

His pushback about my interest is unsettling to me, and I can't tell if he's threatened by my being an attorney or that I'm a civilian who has the nerve to question the military courts. "I'm interested because I've known Izzy—I'm sorry—Isabella for years and she's not the type of person to shoot down a bunch of innocent civilians. Plus, she called me and asked for my help. She doesn't do that very often so I figured it was probably important that I show up."

Opening his eyes wide in complete dismay, Tom clears his throat before responding to my answer. "Well, um, what would you like to know?"

"Why have you not filed a request to get her out those dreadful clothes and get her in some proper attire?" I ask, refusing to give him some softball questions first. I'm only here for a few days and I don't have time to bullshit or dance around the facts.

"I will. I—I just haven't gotten around to it yet," he stammers. "What else, Miss Hartwell?"

Cuing up for my next question, I focus on Tom's body language. He's trying to remain calm and seem helpful, but subconsciously he's tense and annoyed. Every few seconds he's sighing, cracking his knuckles, and pursing his lips. It's obvious he doesn't like me being here, and it's pissing him off that I'm so inquisitive. "I read over the charge document before I drove here from San Francisco, and was–"

"How did you get a copy of the charge document? Those are supposed to be confidential, meaning only people involved with the Department of Defense can see them." His eyes are wide with rage, and I've clearly struck a chord.

"I have my sources, Mr. Braseford. Anyway, as I was saying, I noticed that Isabella was being charged with a number of article violations, including murder in the first degree. If she were to be found guilty, what kind of time could she be looking at?" I ask, wondering what the worst case scenario might be.

Taking another sip of his coffee, he wipes his mouth with the back of his hand before giving me the answer I'm craving. "Actually, if your friend is convicted, she won't be receiving time at all. She will be receiving the death penalty."

Hearing the words "death penalty" gave me whiplash. *My friend could be put to death for something she claims she didn't do?* Of course, as a lawyer, I'm used to people who have been accused of a crime to deny any wrongdoing, but Izzy wasn't that type of person. She's a sweet, gentle woman who only joined the military because it is a family tradition. I always felt she was out of place in the Marines, and would often ask her why someone like her would enlist. She would just smile before telling me that she strives on tradition and that since she was an only child, it meant the world to her father that she wanted to be of service to the American people. While I couldn't see where she was coming from, considering I joined the Marines purely out of spite, I respected her choice and was happy that I got to serve my country beside her.

Thinking about the lengths Izzy went to in order to make her father proud, I start to think about my own. *What would he say to me in this situation?* My mind transcends to my teenage years when he and I would have heart-to-heart conversations at the dinner table while he helped me with my homework. I recall asking him one time what was more important, friends or success? My dad looked me right in the eyes, and with a serious face, he told me, "Maya, jobs come and go. If you work hard enough and prove yourself to be valuable and reliable, you can easily go out and find a new one at the building next door. But, a good friend, those are hard to find. You can't just go to the next person and assume they will be respectful, loyal, and supportive. So to answer your question, friendship is always more important."

With my father's words ringing in my head, I take his advice to heart and tell Tom what I want him to do. "I need you to make me second chair for this trial."

The attorney scoffs at my request, as if he thought I was trying to tell him a funny joke. But when he looks at the stoic expression on my face, he can see that I'm as serious as a heart attack. "Miss Hartwell, getting the Department of Defense and the U.S. government to agree to you, a civilian, being Isabella's attorney is harder than you think. I understand that you were once in the military, but the courts here aren't the same as they are in San Francisco. A lot of the information and evidence given is classified, which is one reason the trial isn't being televised."

"Look, I'm just trying to ensure that my friend gets the best defense available so I'm offering you a helping hand. I get that most of the details given in court will be classified, I really do, but I wouldn't be able to live with myself if I didn't at least try to put my legal expertise to good use." Keeping my stone-faced expression, I pray that he agrees to at least make an attempt to ask if I'm allowed to join the defense team.

Shaking his head, doubt is smeared all over his face, but I can't tell if it's aimed toward my abilities as a lawyer or whether bothering to ask would only be a waste of his precious time. "I guess I could see what I can do, but I'm not promising anything so don't get your hopes up."

"I won't, thank you. So, who's prosecuting the case?" I ask, wondering who I will be standing toe-to-toe with if I'm allowed to sit second chair.

"Major David Laynard," Tom states matter-of-factly, but the slight undertones of that lingering doubt makes me question if I should be worried.

Hoping my assumptions are wrong, and that wasn't a small amount of fear in his voice, I ask, "Is he good?"

Nodding his head, Tom responds with a short but to the point answer, "The best."

"How about you, Tom? What's your batting average look like in the courtroom?"

"I do okay. Depends who you talk to I guess." I can see the words leaving his mouth, but his eyes are telling a completely different story.

Not wanting to pry, but feeling I should get more insight on the man who will be defending my friend's life, I ask a follow up question: "Have you ever won a case?"

The way he looks away and focuses on something else, I already know his answer before he says it. "No, not yet."

Repressing my outrage and shock, I take a page from his book and look around the room so my face doesn't give away what I'm thinking. "How many cases have you worked on?"

"Including this one?"

"Yes," I respond, praying to every God of every religion in the world that Izzy's case is not his first. If it is, I would already know that this entire situation is a cover up. The best way to cover your ass and send a scapegoat to death would be to give them a rookie lawyer with no experience. It's almost a guaranteed guilty verdict.

Luckily, his answer isn't what I dreaded the most. "This will be my third."

His answer makes me feel a little bit better, but only because I remember how hard my first handful of cases were. Each trial had its own set of hoops I had to jump through, and it wasn't until around my tenth case and subsequent trial that I finally found my groove. However, I was much younger back then and fresh out of law school, which makes me wonder how long Tom has been practicing law. Although I don't want to come off too nosy, I ask him a question and hope that it doesn't rub him the wrong way. "How old are you, Tom?"

Looking back-and-forth as if he's calculating the years he has been on this Earth, he decides to go against the quantitative norm and responds with, "I'm older than I look."

He may not have given me the answer I hoped for, but I'm not going to keep asking him personal questions when there is more at stake than how close Tom is to collecting a Social Security check. Letting out a sigh, I remember something I may need if I'm allowed to sit second chair. "Am I going to need security clearance for the plea part of the trial?"

Pursing his lips and shaking his head, Tom gives me a definitive answer. "No, only for any classified parts of the trial. But as you are an ex-Marine that shouldn't take long. I can just make the request when I ask about you joining the defense team. Kill two birds with one stone, you know?"

Standing up from my seat, I pull a business card out of my pocket and hand it to him. "This is my card. It has my cell phone number and email on there. Let me know what the decision is either way. Day or night, it doesn't matter. I always have my phone on me."

Chucking the card on top of his small stack of case files, he nods at me before turning to his computer. "Will do. Thanks. Oh, and before you leave—" he begins to say, "What hotel are you staying at? You know, in case I have to send any file or reports your way."

His question throws me off for a second, mostly because we will be working together closely and possibly seeing each other every day. However, it isn't even close to the realm of the strangest questions I've been asked and I normally extend the courtesy of giving my address to other attorneys I'm working with. There have been times that a major development has been made in a case I was working on, requiring a messenger to drop the documents off to me at my home. Pulling the keycard to my hotel room out of my briefcase, I read the room number off of the small paper jacket folded around it. "It's the Marriott, the one that's a couple blocks down, right off the highway. Room 117."

Tom jots down the information I gave him and turns back to his laptop, essentially excusing or dismissing me without saying a word. I exit his small office building the same way I entered and close the door behind me, dancing inside, that I may have a chance to help Izzy and prove to the world—primarily the U.S. Marines—that my friend would never do something as heinous as the acts she's being accused of.

The moment I get into the car, the full impact of my stressful day hits me like a ton of bricks. Between the long drive, my visit with Izzy, and my impromptu meeting with Tom, I'm exhausted in every way possible. I've never been a fan of going to sleep early, especially when something stressful in my life is going on, but right now I can't wait to climb inside that king sized bed back at the hotel and go to sleep. Getting into my car for the last drive of the day, I make the 15 minute trip to the hotel but decide to make a quick stop at the diner next to it. Sometimes I forget that food is essential and I have to eat if I want to stay alive. My brain had been so focused on everything else except for my bodily needs today, and now that I was ready for bed, my stomach was making me pay for my absent-mindedness.

After gulping down a large plate of pancakes, eggs, bacon, sausage links, and two slices of peach cobbler, I climb back into my car and drive to the next parking lot. Coupling my previous fatigue with my pending food coma, I make my way through the sliding glass doors and push myself to keep moving until I can collapse on the downy-feather comforter. Luckily, my room is on the first floor so I don't have to climb up any stairs due to the elevator being out of order.

Slowly walking down the long stretch of hallways, I reach the last room on the right, slide my key card into the door, and push it open. Taking a quick look around, I can't help but notice that the room is in shambles. The bed is messed up, the pillows are all over the floor, and all of the drawers are open. *What the hell?* Walking back out into the middle of the hallway, I look to the left and right of me to see if anybody who works here may be around.

Further down the hall, one of the housekeepers is backing out of a room, pushing a cart full of dirty towels with one hand and pulling a large vacuum behind her with the other. No longer tired as I had been a few minutes ago, I jog toward the woman and call out to her as I approach. "Excuse me. Ma'am?"

The housekeeper looks over at me with annoyance, and I can only imagine what she thinks I'm going to ask her. Knowing what goes on in hotel rooms and what the maids are forced to clean up when people leave, I too would probably be annoyed if I were her. "Turndown service is available at eight p.m., no sooner." She responds, unwilling to give me a chance to tell her anything else.

"No, no. I'm not asking for a turndown service. I had checked in earlier and had only been in my room long enough to put my stuff down before I headed out to a meeting. But when I just walked in, the room was destroyed. I'm in room 117. Do you know what happened?" I ask, wondering if she may have seen anyone walking out of the room while I was gone.

"Room 117... 117... 117." She repeats, tapping her chin as if she were trying to remember. "Oh, right. I went to knock on the door to see if you needed any fresh towels, but the doorknob had the 'do not disturb' sign hanging on it. I went back later and it was still on there, up until about a half hour ago. I was just about to circle around and try to knock on the door again before my shift ended. But if you're asking if I had seen someone around the room, I haven't, sorry. Have you been robbed, miss?"

"I'm not sure. I'll look through my things and see if anything is missing. Thank you for your help." Scratching my head, I walk back to my room. Without a doubt in mind, I know that I didn't hang that sign up. That only leads me to believe that someone broke into my room at some point today, and I can only hope that they didn't steal anything.

Locking the door behind me when I get to my room, I begin to put the room back together and figure out what someone may have been looking for. Sitting on the bed, I look around the room one more time. *None of my belongings are out of the bag and it's still zipped up, so they most likely didn't go through my things.* Deciding I won't know for sure until I check my luggage, I extend my arm out and pull the bag over to me before picking it up and putting it on the bed. I put my hand on the bottom of the bag, but the slider isn't there, nor is there one at the top. Standing up, I look for the small, metallic pulls but find both of them pushed together in the middle of the zipper.

Slowly opening the bag, all the information Wren had sent me regarding Izzy's case was strewn around, a picture of five dead Afghan civilians lying directly on top. I know for a fact that I had put all of the papers inside of a manilla folder and placed it underneath my clothes. I had brought them along on the off chance that I would have some time to look over the information and see where the police were wrong. Moving my clothes around, I look for the folder the papers had been encased in but it's nowhere to be found. *Whoever broke into my room is obviously trying to rattle me, but they are underestimating who they are dealing with. I don't scare easily, never have. The people of Landsfield Ridge can testify to that one. No matter what they threw my way. I pressed on, determined to investigate. Maybe that's why Wren and I got along so well, because we both refuse to give up. That, and the fact we were both treated like "outsiders."* Grabbing a paperclip from my briefcase, I put all of the papers in a pile and slide the metal piece on top to keep them together before placing them back in the bottom of my bag.

Refusing to let this invasion of my privacy freak me out, I grab some clothes and wash the layers of sweat off my body that accumulated from the drive and sitting in the stuffy prison waiting room. Today did not go as planned, and I have a feeling that the rest of my time here might be just as complicated.

Chapter 6

The shrill ring of my cell phone brings me back to reality. As I open my eyes, the sunlight blinds me and I instantly curse having an East facing room. Then, it hits me that I must have dozed off at some point during my brainstorming session last night because I'm still laying on top of the comforter. *Wow! I must have really been tired.*

Realizing my phone is still ringing beside me, I bring it close to my face and wait for my eyes to focus. Although a name doesn't appear on the screen, the area code states it's a San Diego number and I can only assume that it's either Tom or Izzy calling me. Pressing the big green button in the middle of the screen, followed by the speakerphone button, I greet the caller. "Hello?"

"Sorry, Miss Hartwell, did I wake you?" The deep voice asks, concluding that it was not Izzy calling me. Her voice is way too high-pitched, even when she's overtired and stressed out.

"No, Tom, I've been up," I fib, fighting back the yawn that's trying it's damnedest to escape from my body. "What's going on?"

"I just wanted to let you know that you've been cleared to sit second chair during the trial," he informs me, his voice just as flat and emotionless as when I was speaking with him at his office. If he's happy about having another person on his team, there would be no way to tell.

"Awesome! That's great news!" I exclaim. "When would you like to get started on the prep work?"

"Yeah, see, that's the catch," he draws out, and I already know I'm not going to like what he is about to say. "Due to the seriousness of the case, the trial date has been moved up."

"What do you mean 'moved up?' When does the trial begin?" I ask, outraged that the short amount of time I already had to prepare for trial and get up-to-date on the facts has now been cut down even more.

"Tomorrow?" he responds, his answer more of a question than a concrete date.

"Tomorrow?! That only gives me twenty-four hours to get up to speed on all the facts, read up on the witnesses, and find ways to explain the evidence. The logistics alone takes hours of prep work!" Although I know he is merely the messenger, I feel like I could just kill him right now. Just because Izzy is a Marine doesn't mean that the court can take the right of a speedy trial so literally and cut down any chances she has of having not only fair, but adequate legal representation.

"I know, Maya, but I have no say in the matter. All I can tell you is to get over to my office as soon as you can so I can start breaking the case down for you. I'll even make copies of the witness list and the evidence so you can read them over tonight. Okay?" Even when he's trying to extend a professional courtesy, Tom still sounds like an ass. But since I'm stuck working with him, and I had managed to talk my way into being assigned second chair, I have no choice other than to swallow my pride and play nice.

"I'll be there soon. Thanks, Tom." Hanging up the phone, I hop out of bed and throw on some clothes. Knowing I'm going to be sitting down, staring at case files for hours on end, I decide to wear a nice pair of slacks and plain black blouse. I'd much rather be wearing a pair of fuzzy pajama bottoms and a baggy T-shirt, but I want to gain Tom's respect and that outfit doesn't really inspire confidence in my ability to win a case.

This whole situation leaves me with a weird feeling in my stomach and a sour taste in my mouth. I've never been under such a tight deadline to prepare for a case, especially one of this magnitude. From the outside, the only explanation behind the case being moved up is that it is, in fact, a frame job. Trying to keep my head in the game, I push away my worries and finish getting my stuff together to leave. Sliding some flats onto my feet, I grab my purse, keys, and briefcase before heading toward the door. But stop for a second and grab the "do not disturb" sign off the TV stand, sliding it into my purse. *Good luck trying to break into my room again!*

Just as I place my hand on the knob of the door, it begins to jiggle. I step back and watch the door for a second, making sure I'm not imagining things. Just because I made the decision not to let the uninvited guest rattle me yesterday, doesn't mean that my brain didn't make other plans. Suddenly, the door opens a crack, but stops when the chain connecting the door to the frame refuses to allow it to open any further.

A gulp escapes from my throat when the door closes just as quickly as it opened, followed by the sound of footsteps hurrying away. If I had never been in the military, my body would be frozen in place right now. Instead, my head is screaming at me. *There's no time to be afraid, Maya! You are a Marine dammit! Open the door and see who the hell that was. Hurry before they get away!* Following my own directions, I take the chain off the door and fling it open, rushing into the hallway to see who's out there.

A family of four spin around, wondering what's going on, a look of guilt on the father's face.

"Hey, sorry about that. My kid was talking to me and I wasn't paying attention to the room number. I apologize if I scared you."

Waving off his apology, I let out a fake laugh. "Oh, it's fine. Don't worry about it. It was just an honest mistake."

Putting his hand up to say goodbye, the man grabs his young son's hand and unlocks the door of the room next to mine. The little boy looks back at me before he goes into the hotel room, and I give him a smile. I would've waved but my hand hasn't stopped shaking from the adrenaline coursing through my body, and the last thing I want to do is give into the idea that someone may be watching me.

My gut is telling me that I could be in danger, but my head is fighting against it. *I refuse to be scared by some jerk with too much time on their hands. Sure, them going through my stuff could've been seen as a threat. They could have left that picture on top of the file to warn me the same thing could happen to me if I decide to work on Izzy's case. But I don't know anything for sure yet, so what is this person so afraid that I'm going to find?*

Chapter 7

Trying to keep my cool, I get in my car and drive over to Tom's office. Although I'm pretty vigilant on most days, paying attention to what's going on around me, I'm extra cautious today. The short trip over to the office is filled with quick glances in my rearview and both side mirrors, memorizing license plates on the off chance I see them follow me, and taking extra and unneeded turns. I know I'm probably being ridiculous, but seeing as how I have no clue as to who broke into my hotel room, I'm not risking someone tracking me down like a wild animal.

Pulling into Tom's small driveway, I climb out of my car and keep my head on a swivel as I walk onto his porch. Tapping on the door a few times, Tom flings open the door haphazardly and walks away, his phone pressed to his ear. "Alright, I gotta go. The woman I was telling you about just got here. Yep, bye." Hanging up the phone, he sets it on the side of his desk and smiles at me as if I hadn't heard what he said. I try my best not to worry about what others think about me. Being an attorney tends to make people think the worst about you already; like my law degree makes me entitled to their money or something. But considering the fact that I'll be working side-by-side with this guy to keep my friend from receiving the death penalty, I'm curious as to what he was saying about me to the person on the other end of the phone. Tom claps his hands and raises his eyebrows in exaggerated excitement. "Okay, Maya. Are you ready to get started? There's a lot of information, statements, and evidence to go over in less than twenty-four hours."

"I wouldn't be here if I wasn't ready," I reply, before realizing how passive-aggressive I may have sounded. "Um, yeah. I'm ready to get started. Thank you."

"Alright, cool. You can follow me to my conference room, I have everything all set up for you." Signaling for me to follow him, he leads me down a small hallway and stops in front of a closed door at the end of the hall. "Now, just so you know, my conference room is pretty small. But feel free to spread out everything so you can look it over."

Pursing my lips together, I give him a nod. "Thanks for the warning. I'm sure I'll be fine."

When he opens the door, I see that he wasn't kidding. The room is pretty small, and reminds me of a jail cell without the bars. It couldn't be any larger than ten-by-ten square feet, with a long, wooden table placed in the middle of the room and chairs surrounding it. On the side of the table, sits a stack of files at least two feet tall. I try not to gawk at them, but the amount of work that needs to be done in such a short amount of time seems unreasonable. Pushing away the negative, yet rational, thoughts, I take a seat at the conference table and start getting to work. I take the first case file in the stack and begin to spread out everything one folder at a time.

"Alright, Tom. Give me the highlights. What am I looking at here? What is the Prosecution trying to say?" I ask, hoping to get a leg up if I know what I'm looking for.

Tom sits beside me, takes a sip of his coffee, and begins to break it down for me. "Well first of all in a military case we do not have a Prosecution they are called 'trial counsel'. So, all the Trial Council's witnesses have the same recollection of the incident, but I can't help but think that all of the reports they gave sound suspicious. It's almost as if they had been coached and told exactly what to say. But the most damning evidence—and what they are really using against Isabella—is the rifle camera footage from her M16A2 gun. I'm not sure if you used the same technology when you were in the service, but the rifle cam is enabled when the gun's safety is off and in the horizontal position. All of the footage from the gun's cam videos are encoded with the name of the Marine that the weapon is issued to. Unfortunately, the footage shows that it belongs to Isabella's weapon."

"Okay, but footage can be faked or forged. That's the main purpose behind Photoshop. What is the Prosecution I mean Trial Council trying to say what happened? Why would Izzy, I'm sorry, *Isabella* kill those people?" I ask, wanting to know the explanation that would be provided in court so I could find a reasonable counterargument.

Clearing his throat, Tom explains the case to me. "So, the scene of the crime took place in a village on the outskirts of Kandahar in Afghanistan. The group of Marines Isabella was assigned to, arrived at the village due to the intel they received, which stated the Improvised Explosive Device—IED in case you forgot—that killed some of the men from their platoon three weeks earlier was made in the village. The platoon's job was to go there to see if they could find any supporting evidence. Anyway, the Trial Council is stating that as the troop was approaching the village, Isabella told her commanding officer that she needed to go to the restroom urgently. She went off around the corner of the building for privacy. While the team patiently waited for her, they heard shots being fired. They raced around the building, but she wasn't there. They ended up finding her inside the building firing off her gun, emptying the magazine, and some people dead on the floor. Her commanding officer took the gun off of her, and she started screaming like a banshee when they tackled her to the ground. Supposedly, it took three of her fellow officers to subdue her."

I listen to what he is saying, but I still don't hear the answer to my question. "Okay, that's all fine and dandy, but where's the why? What's her motive behind the attack?"

Shrugging his shoulders, Tom responds half-heartedly, "That's unknown as of right now. I'm assuming they are going to go with the fact that Isabella's boyfriend was one of the men that was killed by the roadside bomb. That's the only explanation I can think of. Maybe they are going to try to sell the story that she was acting out of revenge."

"I can see how the story seems plausible," I tell him, nodding my head as I go over their story in my head. Turning my attention back to the mountain of paper in front of me, I ask, "So what angle are we working on here? She was able to tell me some of the story when I visited her but then the guards interrupted and took her away."

Looking kind of surprised by how my visit with Izzy ended, Tom slowly begins to explain our game plan. "According to Isabella, as the platoon was approaching the village, they stopped driving. She was asked to get out and protect their flank, but wasn't told anything else. She watched her troop walk around the building where the shooting occurred while maintaining a watchful eye on her surroundings. Fifteen minutes later, she heard shots but stayed put because she was told to stay in position over the radio. Ten minutes later, when the other soldiers came back, she was asked what the shots were and where they came from. When she responded that she didn't know, they then grabbed her, threw her to the ground, and tied her up. Isabella kept asking what was going on but they refused to give her any answers. She wasn't aware of the accusations against her until she was waiting for her flight back home."

Listening to the terrifying details of what Izzy went through, I can see why Izzy is so afraid of what is going to happen to her. This case makes her look crazy and guilty. Trying to stifle my gulp as I begin to speak, I give Tom my conclusion on the case, "So, if I'm going by Isabella's claims, she might actually be the scapegoat in this case and they plan on killing her to keep her quiet."

"Exactly. It definitely doesn't look good for her." Tom checks his watch and jumps up from the table, running from the room and returning a couple of minutes later. "I apologize, I completely lost track of time. I have a meeting with the judge regarding Isabella's indictment and, unfortunately, I still have to get permission to get your clearance so we will have to conclude this little pow-wow. I did, however, make copies of everything for you so you can familiarize yourself with the case. The first file is the witness list, where you will find all the information on the first witness due to take the stand tomorrow, Sergeant Morgan Wellbeck."

I nod my head that I understand when my phone begins to buzz inside the pocket of my briefcase. Sliding it out of its temporary restraint, I unlock my phone and hope the message is from one of the witnesses I haven't been able to get ahold of for my case back home. Double-clicking on the email icon, I glance at the new message from a screen name I don't recognize. *Who the hell is that?* Most people won't open a correspondence from someone they don't know, thinking it's probably spam or virus infested, but I tend to get a lot of emails from people I don't know due to being a lawyer and my former clients passing my name along to their friends who need a good attorney.

Clicking on the message to open it, the remnants of any hopefulness slowly disappears from my face as I read its contents:

Ms. Hartwell,

Please pay attention because I am not going to repeat myself. Everything you know and have heard about your father's death is a lie. His death was no accident and I have a video of him to prove it. He was murdered.

Sincerely,

Concerned Citizen

Unable to take my eyes from my phone screen, reality only brings me back to life when the screen shuts off. Looking back up from the device, I see Tom staring at me, a hint of concern on his face.

"Are you okay, Miss Hartwell? You look like you've seen a ghost." Reaching over to his side, he grabs a water bottle from the case on the floor. Tom unscrews the lid and hands it to me, watching me intently as I take slow sips from the small opening of the plastic bottle.

"Yeah, sorry. I'm fine," I tell him, hoping I sound convincing enough for him to drop it. Clearing my throat, I put my hands out so he will give me the case files. "So, you said the first witness of the day is Sergeant Whalebeck?"

"Sergeant Wellbeck," he corrects. "But yes. Are you sure you're okay?" he asks one more time as he hands me the stack. Once I give him an assuring nod, he gives me directions. "We both need to be at the courthouse at seven forty-five in the morning. Isabella's case is the first one on the docket."

Still trying to hide the surrealness I'm feeling from the email, I simply repeat what he said to me. "Seven forty-five, first case on the docket. Got it."

My initial thought is that the military is trying to distract me from the case but I soon dismiss this, as the email has a ring of authenticity which worries me. Pushing past my own set of worries, I focus on what's in front of me as I grab my briefcase off the floor and throw it over my shoulder. I hold my car keys in one hand and carry the case files in the other as I make my way to the door. My body must have been swaying even though I didn't notice it because Tom quickly rushes over to me and places his arm around my waist to steady me. He walks me out to my car, opening the door for me and watches me turn on the ignition. Standing next to my vehicle, Tom doesn't budge until I safely back out of the small parking lot and put my car in drive.

Although our little meeting, or "pow-wow" as he called it, seemed to be going well in the beginning, I have a feeling that my reaction to the email may have destroyed any amount of confidence he had in me. Hopefully, I didn't lose the respect he had for me, even if it was just in a professional manner. I want him to feel confident with me as his second chair because I can tell by the amount of evidence that Isabella is going to need all the help she can get.

Chapter 8

As I sit at the small table in my hotel room, looking over the witness list, I find it hard to focus on the paperwork in front of me. Every few minutes, I catch myself sneaking onto my phone and reading over the email I received. Needing to place all of my attention on the matter at hand, I decide to put an end to the madness and get to the bottom of it.

Exiting my email, I go into my contacts and press the phone icon next to Wren's name. I bring the phone up to my ear and listen to the ring as it waits to connect with Wren. After a few rings, his usual happy and enthusiastic voice cuts in, "Maya, I was just thinking about you! Were you able to make sense of everything I sent over to you?"

"Yeah, I did, actually. Thank you. But I actually need your help with something else." I tell him, praying that he won't start to think that I'm simply using him and our friendship as a way to get free research done.

"For you? Anything. What's up?" he asks, ready and willing to assist me in any way possible.

Struggling to figure out where to start, I decide to just rip the band-aid off and start from the beginning. "You know how I told you that my dad died in a car accident?"

"Yeah, what about it?" he asks, intrigued as to where I'm going with the conversation.

"I got an email today stating that my father didn't die in a car accident. It said that he had been murdered. The thing is, though, that it was sent as an anonymous email and the coward who sent it didn't even sign their name. They signed it as 'concerned citizen,' I was just wondering, by chance, that if I forward you the message, you might be able to figure out who sent it. Maybe even do a little digging and see if the email has truth to it?" Even though I know Wren would never turn down a chance to help me, I can't help but feel guilty. Hopefully he knows that I wouldn't ask him unless I really needed to find out the truth, and he's the only person I can turn to. His abilities to hack into computers far surpasses my technological abilities, and he's the only person I know who could handle the situation quickly and discreetly, just like he had with the case in Landsfield Ridge.

"First off, let me say wow! That is insane. Who just emails someone out of the blue to tell them everything they knew about their father's death is a complete lie? But, um, yeah. I can definitely look into it. Just forward me the email and I will give you a call as soon as I find something, okay?" The way he responds takes away a little bit of the pressure the guilt is putting on me, but still, I don't feel good about asking him to do me another favor.

"Again, thanks. I really appreciate all your help, Wren. I'll talk to you soon," I tell him before hanging up.

With the email being taken care of, I put my phone to the side and pick the witness list back up. It's already 10:00 p.m., and I still have so much of this case to look over in order to become familiar with the aspects of the trial. Not to mention, I still have a long list of things to look over pertaining to how the military runs their courtroom and manage to get enough sleep so I can focus tomorrow.

I pour myself another strong cup of coffee and get to work. With every few pages that I scour and absorb the information like a sponge, I pour myself another cup and proceed onto the next pages. After I figure out all of the logistics that my brain can handle without exploding, I take a quick shower and go to sleep, allowing all the facts of Izzy's case to marinate in my brain so I can be prepared for tomorrow.

·········

Waking up to my alarm, I jump out of bed and quickly get ready for my first day in court. Luckily, I grabbed some of my nicest outfits when I packed my luggage, otherwise I would have had to make a quick stop at a clothing store. After styling my hair into a tight bun—just like how I used to wear it during my time in the service—I put on some light makeup and rush to my car. Arriving at the courthouse 15 minutes early, I look around the lobby for Tom and find him standing next to a large set of cherry wood double doors, his arms crossed in front of his body. Moving my way through the crowd of militant spectators and lawyers, I approach him and give him a small smile instead of a glowing greeting.

He attempts to return the smile, but only halfway, with his lips only turning upward slightly. "Good morning," he greets, his tone sounding as if he would rather be sleeping. Quickly checking the time on his watch, he glances over at me again and informs me why he's standing in this spot. "I'm waiting for the guards to bring Isabella to the conference room so I can bring her some decent clothes." He looks down to the floor and nods his head, bringing my attention to the grocery bag full of clothes by his feet. Tom lets out a loud sigh, anxiously checking his watch one more time before he checks his phone for messages. "She was supposed to be here ten minutes ago."

By his tone, I can't figure out whether he's actually tired or just frustrated from the guards running behind. As if someone felt their ears burning, a guard pops his head out of the doors and signals to Tom that Isabella is waiting for him. Mumbling under his breath, he bends down and snatches the bag of clothes off the floor with a small subtlety of rage behind his actions.

Stepping in front of him, I cut him off from entering the courtroom and put my hand out. "Why don't I bring her clothes to her while you take a second to calm down? Izzy's really good at reading people and she will be able to tell that you are pissed off. No offense, but she's probably already anxious enough and I don't think your mood is going to make her feel any better."

Tom takes a second to think it over before reluctantly handing over my friend's clothes. "Fine. Have her get ready and let me know when she's dressed. We have to go over the game plan with her before the case is called."

Giving him a quick nod, I follow the guard through the courtroom and into the conference room where Izzy is waiting for me in the same clothes I made the guards change her out of when I was visiting her. *Of course, they made her change back.* Hiding my own frustrations with the prison, I give my friend a big smile when her eyes meet mine.

"Oh my god! Maya! Thank god, you're here. I was just informed yesterday that you would be sitting second chair. You have no idea how relieved I feel." Izzy gives me a tight hug, wrapping her arms around me and squeezing for dear life as if she could walk out of the courthouse with me if she squeezed me just hard enough. When she lets go, she looks around and allows her eyes to settle on the door. "Where's Tom?"

"He's outside. He will come in after you get changed." It isn't until after I explain to her where her lawyer is that I realize I came into the conference room for a reason, and I promptly hand over the bag with her clothes in it. Izzy sets the bag down and pulls out a set of her fatigues and a pair of combat boots. I'm having a hard time deciding whether Tom didn't know what she should wear so he just grabbed her uniform or if he is using the camouflage outfit to remind the Jury or panel of members as the military call it that she is a respected Marine. I can see it in Izzy's eyes that she is wondering the same thing. Trying to break the tension that is building up in the room, I make a joke in hopes of making her smile. "At least it's in your size."

She lets out a fake chuckle, trying to show me that she appreciates the attempt but I know this is a lot for her to take right now. She's in the fight of her life and is completely void of the energy it takes to actually be able to laugh. Without saying another word, Izzy turns away from me and pulls off her shorts and baggy T-shirt, replacing them with the fatigues she is used to wearing. When she turns back around, I can see the tears building up on her bottom eyelid, clinging to the eyelashes as she struggles to hold them back. Although I try not to think about it, my thoughts wander into the dark corners of my mind, questioning whether the clothes my friend is being forced to wear brings back memories of the day those people were murdered.

I've never seen Izzy cry, and by the way she is trying to remain calm, I know that she is trying to avoid bringing attention to her overwhelming emotions. As much as I want to hug her and hold her as she cries, I respect her decision to appear strong but still give her a minute to collect herself before I let Tom know that she's ready to talk strategy.

Izzy wipes her eyes, gives me a small nod, and an appreciative smile, letting me know she's good. *It's showtime!*

Chapter 9

I step out of the room and wave Tom in, only to receive a huff and an eye roll in return. "About time," he whispers as he pushes past me to walk through the door. We spend the next fifteen minutes discussing strategy when we are interrupted by the court bailiff announcing that our case is about to be called. As a team, we march through the small hallway, turn into the courtroom.

I take a deep breath as I step into the military courtroom, my eyes scanning the room and taking in its stark, utilitarian design. It's a far cry from the plush, wood-paneled chambers of the civilian courts I'm accustomed to. There are no echoes here; I am so use to hearing the sound of my voice echoing back at me in civilian court but this room is designed to absorb sound, to create an atmosphere of solemnity and order. I can't help but feel a sense of reverence as I take my seat at the defence table, acutely aware of the weight of responsibility that comes with this new setting. I know that the stakes are high, and that every word I speak has to be chosen carefully. In this courtroom, there's no room for theatrics or grandstanding. Here, justice is served with a cool, methodical precision. Hopefully I can perform outside of my familiar Room of Echoes.

A few people enter through the large double doors Tom and I had been standing next to less than 30 minutes ago, taking their seats in the gallery. It only takes me a split second to realize that everyone in the audience, watching the case unfold in front of them, are wearing the standard Marine-issued uniform. My eyes scan over all of their faces, seeing if any of them look familiar from the pictures provided to me by the witness list. I feel disturbed when I come to realize that each and every one of the people staring at the front of the room, waiting for the judge to make their appearance, are witnesses in this case.

Leaning into Tom, I whisper, "Why are all of the witnesses present in the courtroom? Won't that taint their testimonies?"

He gives me an annoyed look before harshly explaining the reason. "This isn't like the courtrooms back in your civilian world. They already gave their statements, so that's what we have to go off of."

I can feel Izzy's eyes on me when I sit back in my seat. When I turn my head toward her, she scrunches her brows together and shrugs her shoulders. I don't have to be a mind reader to know that she's asking me what's going on. Wanting her to keep her attention on the trial rather than Tom's attitude toward me, I purse my lips and shake my head, essentially telling her not to worry about it.

Just as everyone in the court's audience takes their seat and gets comfortable, Major David Laynard makes his grand entrance and it seems like he picked a convenient time to enter the room. He acts like he wants to make sure all eyes are on him, so everyone knows that the best Trial Counsel is in their presence and that the Defense team has no chance in hell of winning. As Major Laynard takes his seat at the opposite table, I look past Tom to get a good glimpse at him but I can't help noticing the large amount of sweat dripping down my first chair's face. The realization that Tom already knows we are about to lose hits me fast and hard. *We are already screwed and the trial hasn't even started yet.*

The bailiff walks in front of the large lacquered bench that sits front and center of the room and loudly announces, "All rise for the Honorable Judge Martin."

On command, everyone in the room gets up from their seat, including both groups sitting behind the tables as a man in his late 50s to early 60s exits from his chambers. Judge Martin's white hair appears nearly translucent when compared to his dark black robe, while also making the wrinkles around his eyes and mouth more defined. It's obvious this man has a life outside of this place—one full of happiness and laughter—although the stern expression on his face makes it harder to imagine him enjoying his time outside these courtroom walls.

Judge Martin addresses the room in a carefully modulated, yet rotund voice. "Thank you. You may now take your seats." Upon command, the entire room takes their seat as the judge gets his papers in order. "I understand the Defense would like to address the court before we start the opening statements?" he asks, his eyes still focused on the paperwork in front of him.

Tom raises his brows, thrown off by Judge Martin's question, and turns to me. Refusing to make eye contact with my first chair, I respond to the judge's question. "That's correct, Your Honor."

As I stand up to address him and the jury, Tom wraps his hand on my arm and pulls me toward him so he can whisper in my ear. "What the hell do you think you are doing?"

"My job," I hiss back, matching his tone. "I just have to attempt to have the case dismissed, at least."

"Good luck, I've already tried. Just remember that you are second chair, and you are supposed to run things by me first." Tom glares at me for a split second before he abruptly lets go, leaving small red imprints on my forearm where his fingers had dug into my skin.

Shaking off my rising temper and slight embarrassment, I place my arms behind my back and address the judge with as much confidence as I can muster. "Your Honor, after looking over the facts of the case, I believe that the Prosi ah excuse me I mean Trial Council has built their entire case on nothing more than circumstantial evidence. I am motioning that the court uses this lack of concrete evidence as grounds for dismissal."

Without even looking at me or acknowledging anything I said, Judge Martin looks forward and states, "Motion denied. Is there anything else?"

"Yes, Your Honor. I would also like to ask the court to allow the case be made public, as is Ms. Isabella Martinez-Garcia's right, according to the Sixth Amendment and the Supreme Court's decision in *Ortiz vs. United States*," I cite, hoping to at least get one win today.

Completely unamused by my use of a precedent case, Judge Martin's sardonic expression tells me exactly how he is about to rule. "Miss Hartwell, while I respect the Supreme Court's ruling in the preceding case, this trial will not be open to the public. Not because I don't respect the defendant's Sixth Amendment right but because this case is a matter of national security. You should feel lucky that you were even given access to this courtroom or its records. With that being said, motion is denied." He slams down his gavel, signing off on both of his decisions before motioning for Major Laynard to begin with his opening statement.

The Trial Counsel stands up and straightens his tie, as he walks toward the panel of members box with a sly smile on his face. "Ladies and Gentleman of the jury, you've been selected by the Court Martial Convening Authority because they believed all of you were smart enough to see through the Defense's story and the blatant lies they are willing to tell in order to get their client off scot-free. Scot-free from what you ask? First Degree Murder. The Trial Council will prove beyond any reasonable doubt that Second Lieutenant Isabella Martinez-Garcia was responsible for the murder of not one or two, but *three* innocent civilians in a village on the outskirts of Kandahar on the twelfth of October. The evidence is overwhelming. We have three eye witnesses, as well as video evidence from the defendant's rifle cam showing the blatant disregard for human life as she shot these three people dead. We have the weapon and a solid motive. The Defense will desperately try to convince you that this was a conspiracy involving numerous officers from the marines division. The reason for this insane and asinine conspiracy theory is simple. They are unable to refute the overwhelming evidence that will be presented against their client. As you listen to blatant lies the defendant tells you, you will find that there is no other alternative than to find her guilty of all charges."

Major Laynard takes his seat and takes a sip of water, clearly proud of the work he put into writing his blasphemous statement against Izzy. Listening to him explain why she would kill three innocent people, I took note of two instances that Tom was completely correct about regarding the opposing side's case: The Trial Council was going to use Izzy's dead boyfriend as the motive behind the attack; and Major David Laynard was the best Trial Counsel around.

Judge Martin waits for Major Laynard to settle into his seat before signaling for the Defense to start our opening statement. Tom stands up and tries to smoothly make his way over to the jury, as the Trial Council had, but only manages to appear like he is doing an impression of a baby learning how to walk for the first time. His movements aren't fluid like Laynard's were, they are rough and jagged as if he's putting too much thought into trying to seem confident. Now I can see the possible reasons why he has yet to win a case, but all I can do is hope that he at least gives a decent opening statement so we can start off on the right foot.

Tom's words start off soft but he seems to get his bearings after he thanks the members of the panel for their civic duty. "This is a case of the military looking for a scapegoat to cover up an organized revenge killing of civilians, who they believe were responsible for wiping out one of their divisions. They chose a woman as the patsy as they believe that an emotional woman of her own fruition would take revenge for the unprovoked murder of her boyfriend. They believe that she can be found guilty quickly and the case would then go away. *Poof!* Into thin air, as if nothing ever happened. As if her life or service to this country never mattered. What they did not take into account is her best friend. A well-renowned lawyer with a 100% win rate who always gets to the truth. A lawyer who has fought tooth and nail to get justice for the defenseless victims, like our client. Together, we will prove that this is a widespread conspiracy and that all the evidence being presented is tainted and manufactured. If the evidence seems too perfect, then it is my experience that it is contrived with no place in reality. My client is not guilty and the only reason she is here, fighting for her life, is that she is what they believe to be a weak, vulnerable woman who can easily be pushed around. They believe that she has no backbone and has no will to throw a punch, even when her life and reputation is on the line. Well let me tell you, they have made a big mistake. The Trial Council has forgotten what happens when you trap an animal—even the most gentle one—they would rather chew off their own leg then lay there and accept their death."

Tom takes his seat, and I have to admit that I feel a little more confident in his abilities after hearing his presentation of the case. Now if only he could get his body language to match his words. He looked so uncomfortable in front of the jury, it contradicted everything he told them and even kept me distracted from what he was saying. This is going to be a rat race for sure, the only question I have is: Who's going to win?

Chapter 10

Judge Martin gladly accepts the opening statements when both sides have finished and turns his attention back to the Trial Councils side. "Is the Trial Council ready to call their first witness?"

"Yes, Your Honor." Major Laynard stands up from his chair and announces, "The Trial Council would like to call Staff Sergeant Morgan Wellbeck to the stand."

Moments after his name is announced to the courtroom, the sergeant gets up from the furthest row of benches in the room, and makes his way to the witness stand. He places his hand on the bible and swears to tell the truth, the whole truth, and nothing but the truth. *Yeah, we'll see about that.*

Sergeant Wellbeck takes his seat and clears his throat before the first question is even asked. As I watch Major Laynard get up from the table, the sound of the sergeant clearing his throat is still audible. It's almost as if his throat is working against him, possibly stress induced. *Maybe his own body is fighting to keep the truth inside. If so, that might just give us something to work with.*

The Trial Counsel walks over to the witness stand and gives the sergeant a slight nod as the man struggles once again to clear his throat, repeating the sound two more times before finally letting out a cough.

"Are you alright, Sergeant?" he asks.

The bailiff hands the witness a bottle of water, and after a couple of gulps, Sergeant Wellbeck nods his head. He lets out one more small cough before responding, "Yes, sir. I'm fine. Thank you. My time on tour in Afghanistan has wreaked havoc on my lungs."

Satisfied with his answer, Major Laynard moves away from the witness stand, his arms crossed behind his back. "I see. Thank you for your service, by the way. Now, I'm sure you are aware of the reason you are here today, correct?"

The sergeant sips his water one more time, taking a second before answering Major Laynard's question. "Yes, sir. I'm here regarding the events that took place during our mission in Kandahar."

"Correct. And could you please tell the court what you re-member about the day on the attack of these *innocent* civil-ians?" Major Laynard asks, his sly smile making another unwel-come appearance. Unwelcome to me anyway. I've met lawyers like him before, many of them, and over the years I have found that the only time they smile like that in a courtroom is when they have a trick up their sleeve. A prime example, being Blaine, the man who took my position at the law firm only for me to be given it back after he royally screwed up.

The sound of plastic being crunched echoes through the room, and my eyes focus on the hand Sergeant Wellbeck is holding his water bottle in and then back up to his face. His expression appears as if he's thinking back to the day in ques-tion, but his bodily reaction is telling a completely different story. He squeezes the bottle again, more subtly this time but still noticeable. "Um, sure. We were approaching the village and Second Lieutenant Isabella Martinez-Garcia let Corporal Alves know that she needed to go to the restroom and it was urgent. We stopped and she went off by herself, turning the corner around what looked like an abandoned building. We stayed in place and waited for her but next thing we knew, we heard shots being fired. We thought she might be in trouble so we followed the same path she took. When we came up behind her, we saw her firing off a clip, completely emptying it, and some people lying dead on the floor."

"That sounds terrifying," Major Laynard responds, his voice sounding of mock concern. "Was this type of behavior normal for the defendant?"

Once again, my eyes are brought back to the tension in Sergeant Wellbeck's hand as he gives the bottle a small squeeze before giving his answer. Quickly, I scribble something down on my legal pad, noting the witness' response to each question so far, and pass the pad over to Tom. Upon reading my note, he turns his head to me, squints his eyes, and shrugs his shoulders. It's almost as if he's trying to ask what my point is. Taking the legal pad back, I scribble another note:

I feel like he might be hiding something. Every time there's a question, he squeezes that bottle. You need to ask him some hard questions on cross exam; put some heat on him to see if he cracks under pressure.

Passing the legal pad to Tom again, he reads my notes and returns my suggestion with a slight eye roll. *I'll take that as a no then, I guess.*

Refocusing my attention on the sergeant, I listen to his response. "No, not at all. If anything, the second lieutenant was quiet and kept to herself–especially after Second Lieutenant Miguel Garcia was killed. She seemed to become quite withdrawn afterward. It was obvious that his death took a toll on her. There was a rumor going around that this would actually be her last mission."

Although I know it's pointless, I jot down another note to Tom, telling him that he needs to ask the witness who he heard the rumor from. This is the first time I had read or heard of this information, and it might just be our way in so we can get the truth out of the sergeant. Tom looks down at the note, gives me a slight nod, and looks back up toward the front of the room.

Major Laynard asks his next follow-up question; the look on his face informing me that this one will be the finishing move in this battle between the truth and the lies these men are telling. "And how did Second Lieutenant Isabella Martinez-Garcia react when the rest of your platoon approached her?"

Another crackle echoes through the silent room, preceding his answer. "Once we knew that the gun was empty and she was no longer seen as a threat, one of the other lieutenants and I tackled her to the ground while Corporal Alves disarmed her."

"Did the defendant say anything? Did she try to justify what she had done?" Laynard asks, his tone stating that he already knew what the sergeant's answer would be.

Sergeant Wellbeck's eyes flick over to Izzy but snap forward, almost as if he's hoping that no one would notice. But I saw it, and I noticed the look in his eyes before they darted away. His eyes are strange, as if he knows what he's doing is wrong, but I don't know him personally so I can't be one to judge. "No, sir. She didn't say anything at all. She just started screaming like a banshee once we forced her to the ground. I have never heard a sound like that come out of a human being before. There was a lot of pain in her scream, kind of like one you would expect from a wounded animal."

Major Laynard walks back over to his assigned seat, turns to face the judge and announces, "Those are all the questions I have for this witness, Your Honor."

Judge Martin turns toward our table, nods toward Tom, and addresses the table. "The defense may now cross-examine the witness."

Looking over at me, Tom whispers, "You're up. Show me what you got."

Happy to finally show off my skills in the courtroom, I stand up from my chair and step away from the table. I can feel every set of eyes on me, making my heart start pumping harder, the sound of my pulse beating into my ears. I love this feeling but only because when I start feeling this way, I truly come alive.

However, the Trial Council seems to have a different opinion. The moment I open my mouth to ask the first question, Major Laynard bolts up from his chair and yells, "Objection!"

Judge Martin's head whips toward the direction of the Trial Council, his eyes narrowed in the man's direction. "On what grounds, Major Laynard?"

The man on the opposing side looks over at me, sizes me up, and looks back over to the judge before stating the reasoning behind his objection. "On the grounds that any information stated in this courtroom is confidential. And, although Ms. Hartwell is a former Marine and we are thankful for her service, she is nothing more than a civilian at this time—even if she is working as the defendant's attorney."

The judge's eyes move from table to table, weighing his options. His eyes finally settle on me when he makes his decision. "Unfortunately, Ms. Hartwell, I'm going to have to agree with the Trial Council. Objection sustained!"

With the bang of Judge Martin's gavel, the rug is yanked out from under me and the embarrassment is only made worse when I hear the sound of snickers throughout the room. Slowly, I lower myself back into my seat and watch as Tom stands up to take my place.

Before he takes center stage, he leans into my ear and whispers, "Tough luck. Maybe next time." Tom walks around the table, trying to imitate Major Laynard's confidence but sorely lacking the charisma. "Sergeant Wellbeck, you stated that you heard rumors regarding this particular mission being my client's last. Who did you hear this rumor from?"

The sergeant begins clearing his throat again, finishing off the remaining drops of water in the bottle. When the water fails to do its job, he lets out a whooping cough and quickly pulls a bright red inhaler out of his front pocket. After a couple of puffs, he takes a few deep breaths and proceeds with a short, concise answer, "I don't recall."

Without any desire to follow up with another question, Tom looks over at the judge before heading back to his seat, "That's the only question I have for the witness at this time, Your Honor."

Trying to hold back my own stupefied reaction from the jury, I find myself questioning whether Tom—my first chair—is supposed to be defending Izzy or has switched sides and is now employed by the Trial Council. The way that my friend is squeezing my hand, I'm sure that she's feeling the same way right about now. If the corporal's testimony wasn't damning for her before the cross-examination, it certainly is now.

After Tom sits back down, the Trial Council calls one more witness, First Lieutenant Dan Thomas. Like Sergeant Wellbeck, the lieutenant states the exact same testimony, but he didn't give an inch when it came to showing emotion. In fact, he doesn't bother to look at Izzy once the entire time he is on the stand, making it ten times harder to read him. By the time Major Laynard is done, I am sincerely hoping that Tom will at least show some type of effort, gumption, or balls and cross-examine Thomas. However, he proves me wrong once again by passing up the chance and taking his seat, infuriating me even more in the process.

Judge Martin waits for Tom to sit back down before checking the time. "I believe this is a good place to take a break for today. Court will resume at 0800 hours tomorrow morning." With the crack of his gavel against the top of the wooden bench, the audience in the room slowly begins to disperse, heading out the door as they talk about what happened during the trial.

Tom gets up from his seat, but I don't follow his lead. I'm too angry with the way he presented our case during his cross to get up, in fear that I might just kick his ass up and down the partitions of the emptying courtroom. The guards return from the back of the room, and Izzy stands up so she can be hand-cuffed. My heart drops as I watch this broken version of my best friend being led through the side door of the courtroom to make her exit through the back door. Sadly, I have the feeling that if I don't figure out how to get Tom's head in the game or take matters into my own hands, the last time I see Izzy is going to be in the same manner.

Staring at me as my friend is being taken back to the brig, Tom lets out a small scoff. My head whips in his direction, daggers shooting from my eyes. Now that Izzy is no longer in the room, I don't have to bite my tongue. She's supposed to have confidence in her lawyer's ability to prove her innocence, and he is completely breaking down any bit of trust in us brick by brick.

"What?" I ask him harshly.

"You are too invested in this case. If you looked at it from an outsider's point of view, you would see that I clearly have a plan." Tom informs me matter-of-factly.

"And what plan is that, Tom? To prove the Trial Council's case for them? Because from an outsider's *point of view* that's all I'm seeing," I fire back at him. "What the hell was that up there? You asked Sergeant Wellbeck one question and it was the question that I gave you. And for some reason, you were perfectly fine with his response. 'I don't recall,' really?!"

Letting out a loud sigh, Tom scratches his forehead and looks around. "Why don't we finish this discussion back at my office? You never know who's listening around here and I don't necessarily want to tell you my strategy when there could be prying ears."

Nodding in agreement, I follow him outside and head toward my car, my rage toward him growing inside me with every step. I have never met a lawyer so incompetent in my entire career, let alone one so pig-headed that he doesn't even realize that his job and main priority should be to *represent his damn client!* As I climb into my car, I pull my cell phone out of my briefcase and turn the ringer back on from its previously silent status.

From my peripheral vision, I can see Tom backing up out of his spot and driving away. Placing my phone in the cupholder, I shove my keys into the ignition forcefully. I imagine the small slot is Tom's face and the cut piece of metal is my fist. *Ugh! He's so infuriating!* As I begin to turn the key, my phone starts letting off a loud string of notifications.

Taking this time to cool down before I completely sever Mr. Braseford's head from his body when I get back to his office, I grab my phone and start going through my messages. "Mr. Reynolds, I will call you back later with an update. Wren, same thing. Oh, and another anonymous email. Let's see what 'Concerned Citizen' has to tell me today, shall we?"

Double-clicking the email notification, it opens up and I scan my eyes over the mysterious message:

Ms. Hartwell,

I hope you haven't made the decision to ignore my last email. If so, I have the proof you need that shows your father's death was no accident. However, my help is not free. If you want the information—the details the police missed—you must wire me $100,000 in bitcoin within the next 72 hours. I will send the account information in a separate email shortly. If you so choose not to wire the correct amount before the time is up, I will destroy all of the evidence I have and you will never know the truth. I hope you make the right decision.

Sincerely,

Concerned Citizen

Although it's hard, I move the email to the back burner of my mind and add it to my list of things to discuss when I call Wren later. If I want to prove Izzy is innocent, I have to take my own advice and make sure this case is my first priority. Closing out all of the open apps on my phone, I finally start my car and drive back to Tom's office.

By the time I pull into his driveway, I'm ready to argue with him. Maybe it's just the adrenaline from receiving yet another anonymous email or how incompetent Tom was during his cross of the sergeant, but I know I'm not in the mood to be treated like some legal aid attorney who has no clue what she's doing. I worked my ass off to get where I am today and I refuse to be treated less than, especially by a man who has never won a case.

My hands begin to shake again, a sign that my fight-or-flight has begun to kick in—and I have no intention of running so it can only mean the former. Walking into Tom's office, the shaking gets worse so I shove my hands into the pockets of my blazer before I'm tempted to hit the smug man standing in front of me.

Tom stands there, his arms wrapped tightly in front of his chest, only breaking the connection when he signals to me with a small wave of his hand. "Alright, let's hear it. Tell me what's on your mind so we can get this over with and move onto our strategy for tomorrow."

"You wanna know what I have to say? Okay, well here it is. Your cross-examination of Sergeant Wellbeck and Lieutenant Thomas was a joke! You didn't ask any questions that would dispute the evidence, nor anything that could prove your opening statement–that Isabella is being used as a scapegoat. How do you expect to win the case if you can't even prove your opening statement to be true? I'm starting to wonder if the Marines hired you because they knew you were going to lose, only to make it easier to crucify Izzy. We have a very short and tight time frame so by you not taking advantage of asking questions and dismissing responses when we are cross examining seems ludicrous!" I tell him as I dig my nails into the palm of my hand, the rage I have inside fighting against me and begging to let it all out.

"You mentioned before about me being too involved as she is my friend. Well, yes, you are probably right, but holy crap, this is her life on the line here!" My voice escalates as the feeling of the situation we are involved in gets the better of me. "But I'm treating her the same way I would treat anyone in this position, with some common decency. Isabella, our client's life or death is in both of our hands. So depending on how well we do, depends on when she will go free or to the death chamber. I *mean* the death chamber. I can hardly believe I am even saying these words. This is her one and only chance and it rests with you and I. That performance in there today was nowhere near good enough with what is at stake."

"Well, how about this, Miss Hartwell? If you don't like how I cross examine my witnesses, then feel free to recall them at the end of the trial, before closing statements. Okay? Then you can show me how a 'real' lawyer gets it done. Who knows, maybe you can teach me a thing or two–that is if you can figure out a way to convince Laynard and the judge to allow you to do your job." Tom narrows his eyes at me, shaking his head as if I'm the one in the wrong here. He begins to walk away when the realization of what I said hits him. In one quick move, he spins around toward me and huffs. "By the way, I would never take on a client just to purposely lose their case. Believe it or not, I do have morals."

"God, I hope so. I am a good lawyer but normally only financial compensation is on the line; this time someone's life is on the line, and not just someone, it's my friend–my best friend." I reiterate as I walk toward the conference room, ready to get our strategy for tomorrow prepared so I can go back to my hotel room. The less amount of time I have to spend with Tom in that tiny room, the quicker my own homicidal rage will hopefully subside. And the sooner I can get back to my hotel room and make some extremely important phone calls.

Chapter 11

It's nearly five o'clock by the time I get back to my hotel room, and as soon as I sit down, my phone begins to ring. On my caller ID, Mr. Reynold's name flashes across the screen. I quickly answer the phone, using the most professional voice I can manage, despite being mentally and physically exhausted from the events of the day.

"Hello, sir. I was just about to call you," I tell him, assuring him that I hadn't forgotten about our deal.

"Good afternoon, Maya. I was just calling to check up on you. I hadn't heard from you since you left and wanted to make sure you were keeping up on the preparation for the trial." His voice is calm and low, but I can sense a subtle hint of worry in his voice. Almost as if my short break from the office is going to disrupt my ability to get justice for the victims.

"Yes, sir. I plan on sending out one more round of emails to the witnesses I haven't heard from, tonight. I did, however, prepare subpoenas before I left, just in case I hadn't heard from them. I know that wasn't necessarily a route you wanted to go, but they are all set to be sent out in the event I don't hear back." I inform him confidently, hoping to get his worries to subside.

"Very well. Are you still planning to be back to work tomorrow?" he asks inquisitively. I swear it's almost as if he knows the answer to the question, but is insisting on testing me.

"Actually, sir." I start off slowly, trying to figure out how to explain to him what's going on without him getting upset. "I was assigned to be the second chair on my friend's case. I wasn't really planning on it, but I felt I had no choice once I learned she could receive the death penalty if she is found guilty. I hope you understand."

"I do understand, but as you can imagine I am not very happy with your choices right now. We have a major trial coming up and you are my first chair. How am I supposed to explain this to the clients? What am I supposed to tell them? That you are out galavanting around in San Diego, trying to save a friend while they are suffering from their injuries? Does that sound very professional to you?" His worries may not have subsided, but his calm demeanor certainly has. Mr. Richards isn't exactly yelling at me over the phone, but has managed to make his point crystal clear without having to raise his voice.

Forcing myself to maintain the same confident tone, I try to explain to him the importance of both cases. "Sir, I swear I am not going to fall behind. We will be all set as soon as I get back, and from the way the trial is going, I don't see it lasting very long. There's no need to worry, Mr. Richards. Honestly, after meeting the attorney assigned to my friend, I really didn't feel like I had a choice but to help. That's all I can really say about the case, as many of the details are considered confidential in nature. But, I can assure you that I will keep in contact with everyone involved in the case and I will be back in time for the trial. You know how much being a Senior Partner means to me, I would never do anything to mess it up."

"I'm glad to hear you appreciate your job and are taking this case seriously. I guess I will just call you in a couple of days to see if you have a better idea of when you will be back. How does that sound?" Mr. Richards asks, his tone sounding a little more satisfied than it was a moment ago.

"That sounds great, sir. Thank you." I tell him graciously, happy that he understands why I couldn't stand idly by and watch my friend be sentenced to death because of an incompetent lawyer. Although the firm doesn't handle homicide trials, our glowing reputation comes from going above and beyond for our clients in order to make sure they are given a fair trial. So if anyone understands what I'm up against, it's Mr. Richards.

"Have a good night, Maya. I will talk to you soon." he tells me, bidding me farewell similar to how my father used to. The very thought of my father reminds me to call Wren as soon as I get off the phone with my boss. The newest anonymous email needs to be addressed, and I'm curious to see if the gifted hacker was able to dig up something interesting regarding my father's death.

"Good night, Mr. Richards," I respond, before pressing the large red circle to hang up. Not even bothering to place the phone down, I go through my contacts and click on Wren's name. Pressing down on the screen hard enough that I fear I might crack it, I bring the phone to my ear and wait for him to answer.

"Well, hello. I was wondering when I was going to be graced with your call," Wren jokes, playing coy despite knowing why I'm calling.

"Hi. Sorry, I lost track of time and just got back to my hotel room." I respond, fibbing a little bit. When I had texted him about my trip before I left San Francisco, I had intentionally led him to believe I needed the case files for a new client and left out the part about Izzy being in trouble. For all he knows, I'm currently on a vacation, soaking up the San Diego sun, and enjoying the gorgeous view from a beachfront hotel.

"How's San Diego? Are you having fun?" he asks, trying to make small talk before he starts hitting me with the details he found out about my father.

"Eh, not really. So, you said you found something?" I ask, trying to cut to the chase so I can finally get some sleep. Although it's not my intention to make the call short, the exhaustion I felt when I entered my hotel room is growing more uncomfortable by the second.

"Yeah, I did. Let me grab it real quick." From my end of the phone, I can hear him walking through his house, or wherever he is at the moment, and opening doors. "I forgot that you are never one for small talk." He laughs before letting out a sigh. "Alright, I got the findings in front of me. So, there is good news and bad news. The bad news is that only a superficial autopsy was performed on your father. That concluded your father died from head injuries caused by striking his head on the steering wheel. Due to the collision and not wearing his seatbelt, the coroner was happy with his conclusion."

"I figured that much. What's the good news?" I ask, wanting to just rip off the band-aid so I can figure out where to go from here. That is, if he found the information that will prove my father didn't die from the accident, but was actually murdered. Normally, if this had been one of my cases, I would be five steps ahead and know exactly what I was going to do for every possible situation. However, for once, I'm stagnant and have no clue what to do. This isn't some client I'm dealing with, it's my father and circumstances surrounding his possible murder.

"Well, actually, I'm not sure if this would be considered good news or not, but it is a good place to start. I was able to dig up some threats that had been sent to your father weeks before his death, but in your fathers profession I know this is nothing out of the ordinary. I'm trying to track down any death threats that are more out of the ordinary, but seeing as how he was prosecuting high-ranking members of the Mafia, I can only assume that's where the threats originated from." Wren was right. The death threats weren't technically good news, but at least I had something to build onto. Technically it's a shot in the dark, but right now I'll consider it a silver lining. Something is always better than nothing.

Knowing he probably wants to sit and talk as if we were normal human beings, I don't feel like I have the ability today, as I can feel the bed gaining control over my body and hushing me to sleep. To bring the conversation to a close, I make the decision to agree with him. "I guess you are right. The Mafia isn't known to handle situations like their most important men being tried for federal charges. If you find out any more information just let me know, okay?"

"Of course!" he agrees enthusiastically, almost making me feel like I'm crazy for assuming he wouldn't give me a call if something else pops up.

"Thanks, Wren. I owe you one," I tell him, hoping he will get the hint.

"Actually, Maya, you owe me way more than one. But it's okay. Since you are such a good friend, I've decided to keep a running tab for you. You can close the tab and pay up whenever you have the time," he jokes.

I let out a small laugh, and take in his generous nature before deciding to move on to the next order of business. "In that case, I have another favor to ask. I received another anonymous email today, stating that this mysterious person had proof my father was murdered and would only hand it over if I wired $100,000 to them within the next 72 hours. They want it paid in bitcoin but left out the payment details. In any case, If I don't send them the money, they are going to destroy the evidence. Do you think you could try to track the email down? I'm pretty sure it's the same person who emailed me before, considering they even used the same sign off–Concerned Citizen."

"You're pretty sure it's the same person or you know it's the same person?" Wren asks, giving me a second to think over my answer before explaining. "Emails get hacked all the time, and I know this from experience. For all you know, someone could've hacked your account and saw this as an opportunity for a money grab."

"True," I state in agreement, trying to consider his explanation and wonder if it's an actual possibility. "The only thing I keep wondering, though, is what if this person is telling the truth, you know? What if they have all the evidence and I ignore their email so they destroy it? What am I supposed to do then?"

"I get it, Maya, but I don't want you to jump to any unnecessary conclusions right now. Luckily, you know me and they stupidly gave you 72 hours. That gives me more than enough time to get to the bottom of these strange emails, so I can find out if they are valid or just some asshole trying to extort you for money. Why don't you just relax at the beach, leave all the detective work up to me, okay?"

"Sure thing, Wren. But I gotta get some sleep, I'll talk to you later. Thanks again. Seriously, I appreciate all of your help. You have no idea." After he says goodbye, I end the call and lay down on the bed, staring at the ceiling as I wait for sleep to take over. However, my circadian cycle betrays me and I can't stop thinking about what Wren had told me. *My dad was receiving death threats? Why didn't he tell me? Hell, why didn't he tell anyone? Not to mention, he had Secret Service agents following him around for Christ Sakes, days on end of protection due to who he was prosecuting. So where were they when he received these death threats? Better yet, where were they when he was murdered? None of this makes sense. It's like I have a bunch of puzzle pieces in front of me and none of them connect because they don't belong to the same damn puzzle. Hopefully, Wren figures something out, like if this anonymous concerned citizen's claims hold any merit. Until then, all I can do is wait and place all my focus on Izzy's case.*

Chapter 12

When I wake up the next morning, I feel almost relieved not to have heard anything from Wren. No news means that I can actually place all of my focus on Izzy's case. Well, as much as I can anyway. Trying to fight against the pushback I'm receiving from the Marine's prosecuting attorney isn't exactly what I signed up for. Neither is trying to juggle to get my case for the law firm prepped *and* dealing with this "concerned citizen" person. But, as always, I'll soldier on.

I had lied to Wren when I told him I needed to get some sleep. In fact, I had lied to myself as well. I tried to get some sleep, I really did, but the never-ending questions running through my head made it impossible to relax. Instead, I opened the case file and prepared for today's witness, Corporal Alves.

Looking over his jacket, he might be a tough nut to crack but I'm not worried. Having been in the military, I'm used to dealing with men like him. Strangely, I always found that the bigger they are, the harder they tend to fall. All I have to do is find a good angle to push. In order to find that right angle, I wrote down every question I could come up with that might hit that tender spot. The only thing that could go wrong is if Tom refuses to let me cross-examine the corporal, just like he did when the soldiers of Izzy's platoon were on the stand.

Tom is supposed to be on my team here, but wherever I try to take a step, he seems to get in front of me so I can't move ahead. *I swear, when it comes to this case, if it's not the Trial Council getting in my way, it's the first chair.* No longer willing to give Tom any more attention or my energy, I get up out of bed and get dressed for the day. Pulling my hair into a tight bun and placing a small amount of concealer onto the dark bags under my eyes, I slip my dress shoes on and grab my briefcase before I head out the door. I'm not looking forward to this day in court, but only because I have a feeling it's going to be a repeat of yesterday.

As soon as I arrive at the courthouse, I grab Izzy's bag of clothes from Tom without so much as speaking one word to him and head into the conference room so our client can get ready. There's a strange silence in the room today, almost as if Izzy knows what's going to happen as well. The Trial Council is going to decimate her character and her assigned defense attorney is just going to stand idly by and allow it to happen like he did yesterday. I wish there was something I could say to her to lift her spirits, but considering no one in this case is allowing me to do my job, there really aren't any words that come to mind that will make her feel better.

The bailiff knocks on the door, letting us know that court is ready to begin. Before we leave the room, I take one good look at Izzy, remove a stray piece of hair out of her face, and give her a comforting smile. She attempts to return my smile, but with everything she has been through, the attempt takes too much energy out of her and she gives me more of a grimace.

Unlike yesterday, Tom doesn't meet us in the conference room before we have to march into court, following closely behind the bailiff. Instead, he meets us at the defense table, where he sits there staring at the notes he jotted down on his bright yellow legal pad. *Well, it does appear that he's prepared today. Let's just hope that he actually uses his notes.*

Moments after Izzy and I take our seats, we stand right back up again as the bailiff announces the entrance of Judge Martin. The judge exits from his chambers and takes his seat at the bench, banging the gavel after everyone takes their seats. "Good morning ladies and gentlemen! Now, before we begin, are there any motions or requests that I need to be aware of?" Judge Martin's eyes wander around the room and stop when they reach me, his gaze boring holes into my skin like hot lava. Refusing to take the bait only to be made a fool of again, I shake my head. "Alright, then. The Trial Council can call their next witness."

Major Laynard stands up from his chair, a smug grin on his face, and responds. "Thank you, Your Honor. The Trial Council would like to call Corporal Alejandro Alves to the stand."

As soon as the last syllable of his name is called, Corporal Alves gets up from the back pew of the courtroom and walks toward the witness stand. Compared to his photo in the witness list, Alves looked completely different. It was as if he aged significantly since the picture was taken; however, I know that the military requires photos to be taken yearly in order to keep identification cards as updated as possible. Whatever has caused him to age so quickly must have been stressful, and I am so very interested to know what could have or has happened for him to now be like this.

The Major begins with his line of questioning, "Corporal Alves, it's my understanding that you were the officer in command on the day in question. Is that correct?"

"Yes, sir. I was in charge of the platoon during the operation in Kandahar. We were given the order to investigate the area after intel was received that someone in the village was responsible for planting the IED that killed many members of the previous platoon weeks prior." Alves' voice is confident as he responds to the question, but it almost seems too confident. It's as if he had sat up all night going over what he was going to say, rehearsing his statement until his cadence came across as natural.

Placing his arms behind his back and pacing back-and-forth in front of the witness stand, Major Laynard asks a follow-up question, "What happened when you reached the outskirts of the village? What made the platoon suddenly stop, making it possible for the defendant to open fire on these innocent villagers?"

Alves takes a second to answer, his eyes looking up as if he's trying to recall what he is supposed to say. After what seems like eternity, he finally gives his answer, keeping his eyes on the members of the panel panel the entire time as he recites his statement from his report verbatim. "She said she had to use the restroom. I asked her if it could wait until we were in a safer zone, but she told me it was urgent and she could no longer hold it. Reluctantly, I told the platoon to hold position and watched the second lieutenant disappear behind one of the buildings."

"Had the defendant ever asked to use the restroom before during a mission? In other words, was this normal for her to interrupt a dangerous mission in order to relieve herself?"

Major Laynard asks, pausing in place as he lines up his next question.

"No, sir. Being a married man myself, I know how the urge can come on quickly for some women. Allowing her to break free from the division was my mistake, but I never thought she would take the anger of her boyfriend's unfortunate death out on innocent civilians." Alves states, his eyes moving between the panel of members and Izzy. I can see in the way that he looks at her that there's a sense of sadness and guilt in his eyes.

Guilt over what though? Guilty because he's throwing one of his officers under the bus or because he knows what he is doing is wrong?

I feel the urge to object, but I decide to hold back to see if Tom plans on doing it first. When he doesn't move a muscle, I jump up from the table. "Objection! The witness is speculating, Your Honor. There's no way he would know what was going through my client's head if that's indeed what happened."

Judge Martin stares at me and blinks before responding to my objection, "Overruled."

Slowly, I sit back down and keep my eyes forward, but I can see a smirk fighting to make an appearance across Tom's lips. Major Laynard continues his questioning once he's sure I'm not going to find another reason to object. "What happened next, Corporal?"

"Me and my team waited for her to finish up, when we heard shots being fired around the same area where Isabella, uh, Ms. Martinez-Garcia had headed to relieve herself. All I could think about was that she was in trouble and had possibly stumbled upon an incel who had opened fire on her. My platoon quickly raced over, guns drawn, but found it wasn't like that at all. Isabella was the one shooting, firing off her clip until it was empty." Alves answers, another hint of guilt and distress gleaming in his eyes.

With every question, I notice that Corporal Alves' testimony, along with his voice, gets shakier. Most lawyers may not have noticed the subtle changes in his tone, but I can't look past it. Of course, he could just be nervous about giving his testimony, but my gut is telling me that it's something deeper than that. I could always ignore it, but my father taught me from a young age that my intuition is rarely ever wrong. Taking a legal pad, I scribble down, *Witness is weak. We should attempt to let me do the cross again.* Placing my pen down, I slide the pad over to Tom and tap his arm, but am taken aback when he purposely ignores me.

Trying to brush off his dismissal, I keep my eyes glued on the corporal as his testimony continues. Major Laynard asks his next question, but by the confident smile on his face I already know what he's going to ask. He's going to drive home his line of questioning by discussing the victims. "Corporal, what was the defendant shooting at?"

The corporal straightens up in his seat a little bit, struggling to convey some confidence before he corrects the man asking him questions. "It's more like who. *Who* was she firing at? I wasn't sure why she had unloaded her weapon until I turned around and saw three victims lying on the ground, their bodies bloodied from multiple gunshot wounds."

"Multiple gunshot wounds." The Trial Council repeats, emphasizing Corporal Alves' statement to the jury. As much as I want to look over at the men and women of the panel to gauge their reactions, I fight back the urge. I can always get a play-by-play from the body language expert, whose entire job is to sit in the audience and poll the jury. My only hope is that Tom is smart enough to hire one. Major Laynard walks back to his table and acts as if he is going to sit down before pulling out the classic power move. He stands up straight, as if an important piece of evidence had just fallen into place. "One more question before I hand you over to the defense for cross. Did any of the victims have *any* connection to the group who planted the IED that killed the defendant's boyfriend, Second Lieutenant Marcial Gomez, along with many of his platoon members?"

Alves looks down at his hands shamefully as he answers the question, pulling out all the stops as he reveals the most damning evidence against Izzy. "No, sir. They were... innocent."

"Thank you, Corporal. I have no more questions for this witness," Major Laynard announces as he takes a seat.

Before Tom stands up to cross-examine Corporal Alves, I tap harshly onto the legal pad and demand that he read it. His eyes slowly scan over the paper, then slowly move over to me, his lips showing no color—just deep lines from pressing them together so tightly. He bends down and hisses into my ear once again, "I told you before, Hartwell. If you don't like how I question or cross-examine the witnesses, you will get your chance before closing statements. Don't ask me again until then, got it?"

Tom stands up and puts on his best smile, acting as if he hadn't just reprimanded me in front of everyone, including the judge and jury. After taking a quick sip of water, he walks over to the witness stand to begin with his own line of questioning. "Now, Corporal Alves, you said when you ran over to the area where my client had gone off to relieve herself, she was firing her gun and people were lying dead on the floor. How can you be so sure that she had merely walked into the area and found the people in this manner? Couldn't it be possible that she was trying to ward off the person or persons who had killed them?"

The corporal gives Tom a strange look as he thinks over to answer the question, his eyes narrowed and eyebrows cocked. "Um, that's impossible. She was still shooting at their bodies when I arrived to make sure they were dead. If she was trying to save them, she wouldn't have been firing extra shots into them."

Taking a step back, Tom shakes off the corporal's response before firing off another one. "And what happened after you walked up behind her?"

By the drastic change in Alves' expression, going from haunted when he was answering the major's questions to now quizzical, everyone in the room can tell he has no clue as to where Tom's questions are leading. The first chair on this defense team isn't even attempting to refute the evidence, he's too busy bringing up pieces of the story that will undoubtedly be stated by the rest of the Trial Council's witnesses. "She was still pulling the trigger when we walked up on her, even though the magazine was empty. So, once I realized she was dry firing, I wrapped my arms around her and squeezed so she would be forced to drop her weapon. I then took her to the ground while some of the other men in my platoon held her down so I could handcuff her. She was screaming nonstop. I had never heard those types of sounds come out of a human before, it was scary."

Listening to the corporal's story, I realize there is a slight change compared to the one Sergeant Wellbeck and First Lieutenant Dan Thomas testified to yesterday. According to the sergeant, he and Thomas tackled her to the ground while the corporal disarmed Isabella. Not to mention, the whole in-human scream she let out was mentioned by both of them—almost verbatim. If Tom wants to prove me wrong about his capabilities, now is the time. Surely he's not going to allow the small differences in the story slip through his fingers.

Watching the expressions on Tom's face change from curiosity to indifference, I can't help but wonder if he's going to take this chance to call Corporal Alves out. However, the moment his facial expression stops on one of false confidence and he begins to walk toward the defense table, I know what his final decision is. *Maybe he's just walking back to the table to grab his notes. Please, just grab your notes and ask your next question. I'm begging you.*

Hoping I'm wrong, and that Tom hadn't in fact given up on his cross, I hold my breath as I wait for his next move. But as I sit there motionless, listening to him inform the judge that he didn't have any more questions for the corporal, the breath I'm holding gets caught in my throat. Covering my mouth, I attempt to muffle my cough. Tom looks over at me, a gleam of judgment in his eyes as he takes his seat.

Apparently, I'm not the only person thrown off by how short Tom has cut off his cross examination; however, the opportunistic Major Laynard springs up from his chair. "Your Honor, I'd like to present the court with exhibit A—the footage from the defendant's rifle cam."

Judge Martin looks down at the watch on his wrist, and I can only assume that he's counting down the minutes until he can get out of here, seeing as the courthouse closes at noon on Fridays. He picks his head up and looks over the courtroom before announcing, "Actually, I think this is a good place to stop for today."

"I apologize, Your Honor, but it's only eleven-thirty and the evidence shouldn't take longer than ten or fifteen minutes to present." Laynard argues, wanting so badly to leave this last impression of Izzy on the jury.

Fighting back the urge to roll his eyes, Judge Martin remains professional but responds with a huff. "Permission granted."

I stand up to object, but Tom quickly shuts me down with his hand yanking me back down to my seat. With the press of a button, the visual of three Afghan civilians being shot down plays in front of my eyes. When the tape is over, not a peep can be heard in the room, as everyone sits there speechless and horrified.

Thrilled to receive the reaction he expected, Major Laynard turns off the tape and stands in front of Judge Martin. "Thank you, Your Honor. With that, this concludes the evidence from the Trial Council. The Trial Council rests its case."

As soon as the judge collects himself from the heinous video footage, he clears his throat and flatly states, "We will take a recess until 0800 Monday morning. Defense be ready to present your case." Turning his attention to the panel of members, he reminds them of the rules, "As you have been informed, you are not to speak of the details in this case to anyone for the duration of this trial. With that being said, you are excused and are to report back to this courtroom on Monday morning."

Biting my tongue, I watch as the members of the panel file out of the room and Izzy is taken away by the bailiff. Tom can tell by my pursed lips and standoffish attitude that I'd love nothing more than to rip out his tongue and force him to eat it, but he doesn't say a word to me. I already know he's going to tell me to save my breath and we can discuss what happened today back at the office, so that's what I intend to do.

Chapter 13

When we get back to Tom's office, my hands are shaking with a combination of rage, frustration, and anticipation. I'm ready to get this over with, air my grievances out so we can move on to strategy. Tom must be ready to let me get my grievances off my chest as well, because as soon as we walk through the front door, he takes a seat at his desk and motions for me to start talking.

"What the hell are you up to, Tom? I mean, really, do you even have a strategy or are you just bullshitting me? Because from where I'm standing, it looks like you have absolutely no clue what you are doing up there. I told you that Corporal Alves was a weak witness and you ignored me! Hell, he was falling to pieces up there on the stand and his story has many inconsistencies compared to the Sergeant's, yet you didn't push any further. He even repeated the same exact line about how Izzy's scream sounded, and nothing! You just gave up and took your seat."

Tom looks down at his hands and takes a second to absorb what I have said before he makes an effort to respond. Suddenly, the cocky voice I'm used to listening to is replaced with one of sincerity, throwing me off completely. "Okay, I see your point and why you are so angry with me. To be honest, this is the first time I have had a second chair on a case. This is all new to me, and I guess I haven't been much of a team player. From now on, I'll try to take your suggestions into account and try not to dismiss you so quickly."

Trying to collect my thoughts, I reply with the only words I can come up with. "Thank... you." Realizing how unsure my voice sounded, I shake it off and allow my usual go-getter attitude take over. "Look, Tom, I get it. My being here is hard for you and I'm basically stepping on your toes, but that's not why I wanted to be second chair. I'm not trying to take this case away from you, I'm here to help Izzy and make sure she has the best defense team she can get. That's what she deserves, you know? The point is, I'm only here for a limited amount of time and while I'm here you should utilize my expertise and resources. I promise I'm not here to show you up, but I may actually be able to teach you a thing or two so you can turn your losing streak around."

"You're right—about everything. I did see you as a nuisance and I've looked you up online, you obviously know what you're doing. Why don't we make a deal? I'll do my best to be a team player and will try not to be such an ass if you teach me how to win this case. How does that sound?" he asks, making me wonder if he's actually seen the error of his ways or just trying to butter me up before he shoots me down again.

Hesitantly, I nod my head and agree to the deal. "That sounds great. Why don't we look over the evidence? I read over the transcript of the gun cam and something just didn't sit right with me."

Tom gets up from his chair and leads the way to the small conference room where we have spent a majority of our time while in this office. Knowing how he has the files organized by now, I look towards the pile of reports and evidence against Izzy. Moving the manilla folders around, I cannot find what I'm looking for not without causing a mini avalanche anyways. The folders being so precariously organised on top of each other.

Curious about what I'm up to, Tom walks up behind me and glances over my shoulder. I can feel his heavy breathing against the nape of my neck. As I flip through the papers, the sound of sniffing breaks my focus. *Is he smelling my hair?* Uncertain if that's what he was doing and not wanting to appear rude, I step to the side and place the folder onto the table to sort through the file.

The distance I created between us is short-lived as he moves over to the table with me. "What are you looking for?"

"The transcript of the rifle cam, but I don't see it," I tell him, hoping that he will walk to the other side of the room to look for the document I need.

"Why do you need the transcript? I have a copy of the video," Tom states matter-of-factly.

The admission of having the video footage the entire time instantly infuriates me, but seeing as how Tom's trying to be a team player now, I keep my opinion to myself. Slowly, I stand up and take a deep breath before I say anything cross. "Could you show me the footage please?" I ask, forcing a smile onto my face.

"Sure," he responds, oblivious to the anger I'm trying to suppress. Tom leaves the room abruptly without saying where he's going, but returns minutes later with his laptop in hand. Setting the computer down on the table, he opens the disc drawer, pops the CD in, and pushes the door closed. With the click of the space bar, the footage begins to roll and I find myself watching intently. When the footage is done rolling, I sit there emotionless, not knowing what to say or feel after watching innocent civilians being shot down. Tom takes it upon himself to break the silence, "Did you see what you were looking for?"

"Yeah," I answer, still numb from what I have just seen. "Something doesnt quite add up, I noticed that in the video transcript it mentioned sixteen bullets were fired but I am sure that in one of the witness statements they said the clip had been emptied which would be twenty.

"I mean, I guess." Tom shrugs his shoulders, and I can see that he has no clue what I'm trying to get at.

Trying to be nice and not make him feel inferior, I decide to go a different route rather than breaking it down to him as if he were a child. "What did the video expert say about the footage? Did they verify it and make sure it hadn't been tampered with?"

"Why would I need a video expert to look at the video? I got the CD right from the Trial Council, just like they are required to do. I'm sure they would've known if the footage had been tampered with or not. That would just poke holes in their case." He sounds so sure of himself until he studies my face, and I can see that he is slowly starting to question his own statement. "Right?"

"Tom, they just have to produce the evidence. They don't have to tell you shit about the validity of it. That's up to us to prove." His eyes stare off into the distance, fixated at the wall on the other side of the room, and I'm starting to wonder if I've finally gotten through that thick skull of his. "Why don't I find us a video expert? Do you have a number to one that might be nearby?"

"I don't need a number for one that's nearby. My father-in-law is an expert, in fact every time I read anything about him it reads 'world renowned broadcaster and video engineer', he will definitely be willing to help." Upon hearing this information, I silently begin to pray for the strength and willpower to not give into temptation and strangle the man in front of me. Tom's eyes scour my face for any type of reaction and by the way he pulls his phone from his pocket and begins to punch numbers in, I know he didn't get a reaction that he liked. He walks out of the room, his phone against his ear, and I can hear his booming voice coming through the thin walls. He once again re-enters the room a couple of minutes later, a satisfied smile on his face. "He'll be over in a couple of hours."

Not wanting to take this moment away from him, I offer him a bigger smile, this time showing some actual teeth. "Awesome. Thank you."

Just like Tom said, his expert video father-in-law finally arrives a few hours later, ready to help in any way possible. He's amped up as he steps through the door, his athletic, yet ageing, build and muscular arms prompting me to wonder is he really a video expert geek as his body shape is not stereo typical. But my main worry is will the jury or panel of members as I should call it, this being a military court case, believe he is a video expert when he looks like he spends more time in the gym pumping weights. Marching right up to the table, his eyes are glued to the open laptop screen. But before he sits down, he makes it a point to introduce himself, pushing up his black, thick-framed glasses before flashing me his bright white smile. "Hello, I'm Dr Logan Fellows. I'm what many around this area consider a Broadcasting and Video expert."

Putting my hand out to shake his, I give it a little squeeze and pat. "Nice to meet you, Logan. I'm Maya. I really appreciate you coming over so quickly. We could really use your help."

Logan's cheeks turn red and I can feel the palm of his hand beginning to perspire. Embarrassed, he pulls his hand away and wipes the sweat onto the leg of his khaki pants. "Sure thing.

What can I help you with? Tom didn't really fill me in on the phone, just that he needed help with his laptop."

His cheeks grow more red with every word he says to me, but I refuse to stare so I don't embarrass him even more. Instead, I look down at the laptop screen, the footage still paused at the very end. "I need to see if you can verify the validity of this footage. You know, make sure it hasn't been edited or tampered with in any way. Are you able to do that?"

Letting out a loud huff, Logan follows up with a laugh. "Oh, Maya. That's child's play. Give me some time to run it through my software and I'll have every detail of this footage broken down for you."

Giving him the benefit of the doubt whether its really child's play, I leave the room with Tom to grab some coffees and to give him some space. However, we only get as far as the car before Tom's phone rings with that annoying ringtone theme to Top Gun I believe it is. Its Logan calling us back.

On arriving back in the room with Tom I can see Logan has a big grin on his face.

"Did you find something, Logan?"

His eyes still focused on the screen, Logan responds without looking away for even a split second. "I think so. Well, it might be something. Who's rifle cam is this footage supposed to belong to?"

"Second Lieutenant Isabella Martinez-Garcia. Why?" I ask, the anticipation of what he may have found growing inside of me. Logan takes his time to respond, his eyes scrolling over the screen. Each second that passes by feels like a century, and if I wasn't so worried about hurting my potentially key witness I would knock him off his chair and take a look for myself.

Using the end of his pointer finger to push his glasses onto the bridge of his nose, Logan uses the mouse to highlight whatever he is bringing to our attention. "Well, according to the data attached to this footage, that's impossible."

Logan moves out of the way so Tom and I can see what he found, and instantly my jaw hits the floor. Having a similar reaction, Tom is a little bit more vocal than I am about the discovery. "Holy shit! Do you know what that means, Maya?" he asks, tapping my shoulder in excited glory.

"Yeah, I do." I answer, a smile pulling at both sides of my lips. "It means we just won our case."

Chapter 14

The weekend came and went, and before I know it Monday morning has finally arrived. I anticipated this morning since we discovered the piece of evidence that would prove Isabella's innocence. The whole last minute discovery was actually liberating, and I found myself motivated for the past 72 hours to get as much work done as possible. Not only did I get a long list of questions for my next witness and for the moment I would get to recall the Trial Council's liars–I mean, witnesses–but I also got ahold of all of the people for my case back at home and got them to agree to testify. Needless to say, I feel exhilarated this morning as I get ready for work. The only thing I wish had happened in the last three days was to hear from Wren, but we can't always get our way. I have, however, heard from my concerned citizen friend, who nicely told me that "time was up." At least I know with Wren on it, he can hopefully find whoever is emailing me and shut them down. And if they do have any evidence, get it before it's destroyed.

Pulling my hair out of my face and touching up the dark circles under my eyes with concealer, I'm itching to get this day over with. Even though I'm excited to get this trial over with, for Izzy to be found innocent and set free, and go back to my normal life, I'm a little worried about my first witness. It's not that I'm worried he won't show up, but rather that his naturally nervous nature might make him an easy target for Major Laynard. The last thing I want is for the sharp-witted, and just as sharp-tongued, Trial Counsel to rip the poor guy to shreds on the stand. I can only hope that all the prep work we did over the weekend will work in our favor.

Walking into the courthouse, I flash Tom a big, genuine smile as I grab the bag of clothes out of his hands and march right to the conference room so I can get Izzy ready. She can tell something is up as soon as I enter the room, but for some reason is afraid to call me out on the pep in my step.

"Did you have a nice weekend?" she asks, beating around the bush. Her hands are shaking, and her body language is quite telling. She so badly wants to know what's going on with her case, but I don't have enough time to spill the beans before the bailiff interrupts to let us know it's time to head toward the courtroom.

Instead, I decide to go with a simple, "You could say that."

Right on time, a knock at the door lets us know that it's time to vacate the room and head to our designated seats. Placing my hand on Izzy's shoulder, I give it a comforting squeeze and gift wrap it with a smile. "Let's get this show on the road, shall we?"

Izzy, unsure of what the show is going to entail today, raises her eyebrows as she shrugs her shoulders. "I guess," she mutters, her voice low and soft. Her expression and entire demeanor is one of someone who has lost faith–in the government she had sworn to protect, the judicial system she had once trusted, and, sadly, herself. Although I want nothing more than to give her a big hug and promise her that everything will be alright, we have somewhere to be and the bailiff doesn't really look like the type of guy who likes to wait.

Placing my hand on the small of Izzy's back, I give her a small nudge. I know she's nervous, and likely angry, because all of the people from her platoon who she had trusted with her life are lying about her–in front of her face no less. She would've undoubtedly taken a bullet for any of the men who have testified so far, yet here they are, willing to throw her under the bus. If she were to be found guilty, her brethren would essentially be the ones putting the needle in her arm; and I have no clue how anyone could be okay with doing that to another human being, let alone another Marine.

We take our seats—mine next to Izzy as usual—and I notice right away that my friend's hand is shaking viciously. Placing my palm on top of her fist, I give it a gentle squeeze and lean in so only she can hear what I'm saying. "I know you're nervous, but you don't want the panel of members to see it. Hide your hands in your lap."

Subtly nodding her head that she understands, she places her hands in her lap, interlacing her fingers together in an effort to control the trembling. Seeing as this is her first time being a defendant in a courtroom, I understand why she feels like a bundle of nerves. If I hadn't been raised by a lawyer, I would probably be the same way right now. Except, my hands wouldn't be shaking from anxiety, but of anticipation to show-case my discovery. The entire courtroom stands at attention as Judge Martin exits his chambers, only for us to sit back down and wait for him to speak.

The judge addresses the room, his eyes moving from table to table. "Good morning. We are going to pick up where we left off last Friday. Is the Defense ready to call their first witness?"

Tom looks over at me, a small smile pulling at the sides of his mouth. Slowly, I stand up and announce my first witness. "The Defense would like to call Dr Logan Fellows to the stand."

Just as I knew he would, Major Laynard jumps at the chance to interrupt me. "Objection! Your Honor, I thought we went over this. Even though Ms. Hartwell is an attorney for the defendant, she is a civilian. Also, I don't have any information on this 'Dr. Fellows.' I have no clue who he is or how he is connected to this case."

Glancing over at Tom, he gives me a wink, giving me the go ahead to shut Major Laynard down. We had already calculated this objection into our strategy, and did so by making sure that we forwarded Logan's findings and accreditations to both the Major's and the judge's office Friday evening. Even though Tom is going along with the plan to allow me to take the lead and question this witness, he doesn't really have a leg to stand on. With our active deal in place, the fact that I was the one who found this damning piece of evidence, and I also spent my entire weekend working through every piece I could get my hands on, he already knew I was well prepared and the best lawyer for the job.

Turning my attention back to the judge, I debate Major Laynard's objection with my own justifications. "Your Honor, while I understand that the information in this case is highly confidential, the evidentiary discovery found in the footage of my client's rifle cam was in the possession of the defense team. As Major Laynard stated on multiple occasions now, I am a member of the Defense team. Therefore, the evidence should not be considered confidential in nature."

Judge Martin takes a second to think over my retort, and makes his decision. "Seeing as your argument was well put, and you are technically a member of the Defense team, I do find myself siding with you as far as this objection goes. But please, Ms. Hartwell, tread lightly. Now, as for the second portion of the Trial Council's objection. Who is Dr. Fellows and what part does he play in this case?"

"Dr. Fellows is a video expert. He has been certified by many accredited schools and has worked for the U.S. government on multiple projects. In preparation for today's testimony, I took the initiative to forward Dr. Fellow's findings as well as a long list of his accreditations to both yourself and the Trial Council late Friday evening." Although I feel like gloating as I watch the blood rush to Major Laynard's face as he searches through the case file in front of him and finds the documents, I swallow my pride. The last thing I need right now is the jury I mean the panel of members siding with the Trial Council because they see me as some arrogant bitch. Instead, I stay stoic as Major Laynard lifts the discovery evidence document in the air, motioning that he had found it.

"Okay then; I guess I have no other choice than to overrule the Trial Council's objection." Judge Martin bangs his gavel, sealing his decision, before he addresses me once again. "Dr. Fellows may now take the stand, Ms. Hartwell."

Unlike the witnesses that Major Laynard had called, Logan didn't have the necessary security clearance and was required to sit out in the hall until he was called to testify. Judge Martin motions to the officer standing guard in the back of the court-room, and everyone waits patiently until he appears. Logan enters the room, displaying a sense of confidence as he walks to the witness box, at least he appears that way to the untrained eye. I can see that he is slightly nervous by the way he chews on the inside of his lip as he is sworn in, he obviously understands the gravity of the evidence he is about to give. Never before when he has testified has a woman's life been on the line. So I need to settle him quickly.

After Logan takes his seat, I begin to proceed with my line of questioning. "Good morning, Dr. Fellows."

"Good morning, Ma–Ms. Hartwell," he quickly corrects when he remembers where he is.

" Dr Fellows Please would you state your name qualifications and background and your current occupation "

"Greetings, my name is Dr. Logan Fellows, and I'm a seasoned expert in the field of broadcasting and video with over thirty years of hands-on experience. I possess a diverse academic background, including a Bachelor's degree in Electrical Engineering, a Master's degree in Computer Science, and a Ph.D. in Video Encoding and Protocols from the prestigious University of California, Los Angeles (UCLA).

Additionally, I hold several certifications, including Certified Broadcast Networking Technologist, CBTE Certified Broadcast Television Engineer (CBTE), and Certified Professional Broadcast Engineer (CPBE). Throughout my career, I've held various broadcast engineer positions with leading media outlets such as Fox and CBS, to name a few.

I'm proud to be one of only ten members of the International Telecommunications Union (ITU), a testament to my global recognition as a subject matter expert. My expertise in the past decade has focused on video protocols and analysis, where I've published numerous articles and research papers and provided consultation for several video hardware companies.

As an accomplished expert witness, I've testified in several cases, leveraging my vast experience and knowledge to help the courts understand complex technical issues. Presently, I'm the Head of Video and Broadcasting Standards at Sony US, where I'm involved in developing cutting-edge protocols and standards for the next generation of broadcasting."

I am pleased in he coming across with such clarity and the panel of members are fully engaged. "I think it's obvious but I must ask, do you believe you are qualified to provide expert testimony on the video footage in this case? "

Just as I knew he would again Major Laynard jumps at the chance to interrupt me. "Objection! Your Honor council is giving opinion, "Sustained" the Judge bellows.

"Let me rephrase that. Do you believe you are qualified to provide expert testimony on the video footage in this case? "

Dr Fellow immediately says "Yes" with the confidence of a man who is at the top of his profession

Flashing him a smile, I continue talking, keeping the momentum we have started to build. I want to treble down on his expertise in this field so ask.

"You mentioned the ITU Dr Fellows could you explain what that is please?"

"Yes certainly. It is the main body that ratifies video protocols that is responsible for developing and maintaining standards for telecommunications, including video and multimedia communication protocols.

The ITU's standards and recommendations are widely adopted and implemented by video technology and service providers, as well as by governments and regulatory bodies around the world. As such, the ITU plays a critical role in ensuring that video protocols are standardized and interoperable, enabling seamless video communication and collaboration across different platforms and networks."

"I see, and does that include the protocol of the video from the rifle cam."

"Yes the rifle cam uses mp4 and I was one of the lead engineers in developing and ratifying that protocol."

I believe that everything is progressing smoothly, and since the Prosecution has not raised any objections, or rather, the Trial Council in military speak, they appear to be on the back foot. "Also Dr Fellows do you have any experience of the rifle cam hardware"

"Yes I provided consultancy to the company CJ Halls Inc that developed the hardware so I am completely au fait with the Cam hardware and firmware."

"Now, you were hired to analyze the footage of my client, Second Lieutenant Isabella Martinez-Garcia's rifle cam from her M16A2 firearm. Is that correct?"

"Yes, ma'am." Logan's response is again strong, and I feel as if he is starting to get into the groove of things.

Keeping the energy going, I follow up with my next question. "And what did you find when you analyzed this piece of evidence?"

Logan sits up straight, maintaining a perfect posture as he prepares to enter his realm of computer knowledge. We are in his house now, the place where he feels most comfortable. "After analyzing the video footage from the M16A2 rifle cam frame by frame and passing it through a data analyser, I came to the conclusion that the meta data on the video has been tampered with."

In awe of his further increase in confidence, I keep the momentum going, knowing exactly what the rest of the information is going to do to the panel of members. "Are you saying that the video footage is fake?"

Clearing his throat before he begins to explain, Logan leans in slightly toward the microphone. "Well, yes and no. The video footage is real, very real, but it was manipulated."

"How so?" I ask, eyeing the expression of every member in the panel of members box.

"The data from the Rifle Cam was changed by someone using an editing tool version 2.28 that was supplied with it. This tool could only change some of the information, specifically the meta data on Track one which contains the rifle owners name and gun serial number. However, the updated protocol that is installed in all rifle cams has a second data track called Track two, which contains new data fields that couldn't be seen or changed using the version 2.28 editing tool. So, whoever manipulated the data could only alter the data on Track one but not on Track two.

" Dr Fellows, why was the protocol changed for the rifle CAM? "

"The military were thinking ahead and wanted to store extra data such as GPS positional data, the number of rounds fired etc which is why Track Two was created in the protocol. But as of yet the rifle cam hardware has not been upgraded to make use of this so it just writes a replica of the metadata in Track one which holds the rifle owners name and gun serial number.

"Whoever had changed the owner and serial number data on Track one was unaware that the protocol had been changed. They were also unaware that when the cam is reattached to the rifle and switched on, the data on Track one is immediately copied to Track two as we never like empty data fields. Whoever changed the data had no way of knowing that changing the data on Track one would only get written to Track two when the camera was reattached to the M16A2 rifle. This never happened because the cam was removed from the rifle as evidence. Track one was changed ie the owners name and gun serial number was altered. Then as the cam was never reattached to the rifle Track two kept the original data that had been written to it. In this case revealing the true owner of the rifle."

Liking what I'm seeing on the panel's faces, I hit them with another hardball. "So for those of us who are completely computer illiterate, what does that mean in layman's terms?"

"As I said, the video footage is real; however, that footage did not come from Second Lieutenant Isabella Martinez-Garcia's gun." A small gasp flows throughout the room, almost like the wave you would see at a baseball game. One after the other, the people sitting in the room go into a state of mild shock once they realize what Logan is saying.

Little do they know that this is only half of the big reveal!

Pretending to be just as surprised as the men and women sitting in the room, I cock my head to the side and purse my lips. "Hm, interesting. Well, if this footage wasn't from my client's rifle cam, whose was it from?"

Logan does his best to hide a smirk but is unable to, knowing that his little secret was about to blow the lid wide open on this case. Taking a deep breath, he prepares to leave the audience speechless with his next statement. "When I examined the data, it showed that the data states that the rifle cam video was actually from Corporal Alves' gun."

There is an audible gasp in the courtroom, this one much louder than the last, and if I had a microphone in my hand, this would be the moment I dropped it on the ground and walked away. The gasps quickly turn to murmurs, which become so loud that Judge Martin is left with no other choice than to bang his gavel and yell for order in the courtroom.

Only once the room is quiet again do I begin to feel the tide turning in our favor. Keeping a straight face, determined to hide my glee, I inform Judge Martin, who is still trying to make sense of it all, that I had no more questions for Logan.

Trying to shake off his shock, the judge's voice cracks as he turns to Major Laynard and addresses him. "You may now cross-examine the—excuse me—the witness."

All eyes in the room shoot toward the Trial Council's table, waiting to see what he is going to do with this newfound discovery. Rather than looking around and making eye contact with the waiting audience, Major Laynard stares over the long list of accreditations I had sent him 72 hours ago, presumably trying to find a flaw in Logan's findings.

After a brief silence, it becomes apparent that Major Laynard is struggling to formulate any meaningful questions. It is clear that he does not wish to risk discrediting the expert witness. At that moment, Trial Counsel rises from their seat and addresses the Judge stating, "Your Honor, I have no further questions for this witness. However, I reserve the right to recall a rebuttal witness."

Judge Martin, nodding in understanding, responds simply to Major Laynard's statement. "Very well. Why don't we take a short recess and have lunch? Everyone should report back to the courtroom at 1400 hours." The judge bangs his gavel and the sound of shuffling feet fills the room as everyone begins to file out through the doors in the back.

As soon as the panel of members leaves the room, escaping through a door separate from the onlookers, Izzy turns to me and wraps her arms tightly around my neck. "Oh my god! You did it! You cleared my name!" I try to respond but her death grip on my neck makes it difficult for words to come out. Realizing how her hug was cutting off any means of oxygen for me, she quickly releases me and lets out a little chuckle. "Sorry about that. I should probably wait until I'm found not guilty before I hug you to death."

Softly rubbing my neck as I take in a deep breath, I echo her laugh and give her a thumbs up. "I'm fine, don't worry. And we haven't technically cleared your name yet, there's one more surprise we have in store."

"Ladies, I get we are excited but we only have an hour and a half to eat. I just ordered some food and it's supposed to be delivered to the conference room. Why don't we continue this conversation in there?" Tom butts in, but for good reason at least. Thanks to my excitement to get to court this morning and the adrenaline I had pumping through my system just thinking about the truth being exposed, I completely forgot to grab a bite to eat. My stomach had been growling so loud while I was questioning Logan that I was worried the entire room might have heard the monster in my abdomen begging me to feed it.

As we walk back to the conference room to wait for our food, I hear my phone buzzing inside of my briefcase. Falling behind the group, I motion for them to go ahead without me. "I'll be right with you guys. My phone's ringing and I have the sneaking suspicion that it's my boss wondering when I'll be back."

Izzy gives me a thumbs up before entering the conference room. "Well, in that case, good luck. But I'm warning you now, if you take too long I can't promise that there will be any food left. Prison food is not as delicious as you think."

Rolling my eyes, I wave her to keep walking as I pull my phone out with the other hand. Surprisingly, my phone wasn't ringing because someone was calling me, but rather that I had received a string of emails. Opening my inbox, I hope that the emails are from Wren, filled with whatever evidence he was able to find about the death threats my father had been receiving before he died; but that doesn't seem to be the case this time. When the screen finally maneuvers itself to my email's inbox, all I can see is the same anonymous screen name that has been plaguing me for days–an attachment clinging to every new message.

Wary of clicking on the first picture, I decide to go for it and pray that the attachment isn't some type of virus that's going to shut down my phone or drain my bank account. When the first attachment pops up, I almost wish it had been a virus. Factory resetting my phone would be much easier to explain than what I'm looking at. The image, and every one following, are pictures of my hotel room, the bed, my clothes, and my suitcase. The last attachment hits me hardest of all–a picture of Izzy's case file, pulled apart, just how I had found it the day I arrived in San Diego. *Whoever is emailing me knows where I am–and they have been in my room.*

Chapter 15

Since we are still waiting for our lunch to arrive, I take the opportunity to make a quick call. Scanning through my recent calls list, I stop scrolling when I land on Wren's name. Tapping the screen, followed by the dial button, I bring the phone up to my ear and wait for him to answer. On the third ring, he finally picks up, his usual enthusiastic tone bringing a smile to my face. *Oh my god! Why do I smile whenever I talk to him? He's just a friend.*

The constant flow of thoughts are interrupted when I hear Wren's voice calling out to me from the other end of the phone. "Maya? Maya? *Hello?* Did you butt dial me?"

"Oh no, sorry. I got, uh, distracted. Anyway, I only have a few minutes but I wanted to see if you have been able to figure out who has been emailing me. So, any news?" I ask, hoping that he can tell me something, anything at this point.

"Unfortunately, I don't. Even though my computer skills are above average, possibly even highly superior to other hackers, I haven't been able to track this guy down." Wren's voice changes from energetic and happy to one of guilt, almost as if he feels bad that he hasn't been able to come through on this favor for me. Like he had let me down in some way. "But look, I don't want you to give up on me yet. I've been trying to figure this guy out, there's just so many other cards at play right now. He's making it kind of difficult."

The mention of the particular pronoun he keeps using grabs my attention and refuses to let go. "Wait! Why do you keep saying this guy or 'he?' How do you know they're a man?" I ask, wondering what would make him come to that conclusion.

"I mean, I don't necessarily know. It's just how the emails are written; sounds like they were written by a man–different men at that. I'm just assuming for now until I get some cold hard facts. What I'm trying to say is that the first email you received is blocked by firewalls using multiple IP addresses across numerous countries. His digital footprint is saying that he's in a different country. Hell, sometimes a different continent altogether. I haven't had a chance to trace the subsequent emails you received but I assume they came through the same onerous path. Whoever is blackmailing you knows what they are doing, but that's okay because I'm getting close–I can feel it in my bones. It's become a challenge for me, and we both know how I love a good challenge."

Not wanting to over inflate his ego too much, while also reminding myself that I'm glad he's so confident in his abilities, I egg him on a little bit. "That's true, I have yet to find one that you haven't conquered. But, look, I just received a bunch more emails from Concerned Citizen, and these ones kind of freaked me out. You'll see what I mean when I send them to you."

"Hold on, let me stop you right there." he calls out, a minuscule amount of urgency in his voice. "Don't even bother to forward me the emails because I'm already in your account."

"What do you mean you're already in my account? Since when?" I ask, a tinge of demand hidden behind the question. It's not that I'm annoyed that he hacked into my account, more like, impressed, but considering I use my email to converse with clients, he should have let me know first. The last thing I need is the Bar Association breathing down my neck because someone hacked into my account and read through all of the privileged information I keep stored in my inbox.

"Never mind when, but to answer your question, the moment you said you received another email. Also, I know why you're worried, and just stop. I will remove any trace of my ever being here so the Bar doesn't take away your license. I'm going to go over all of these messages with a fine-tooth comb, and figure it out." The way he assures me makes me feel a little bit better, but I'm still pretty sure that I should ask the hotel to move my room. I wasn't creeped out before when I thought someone broke in, but seeing the up-close snapshots of my panties just makes my skin crawl.

Tom pokes his head out the door and makes the universal motion for "let's shove some food in our faces," prompting me to hurry up and get off the phone. "Hey, I gotta go. Call me back when you get those, uh, documents. Bye!" Hanging up before I give Wren a chance to respond, I slide my phone back into my briefcase and walk into the conference room. "Oh, food's here! Thank God, because I'm starving!"

Nodding toward my briefcase, Tom asks, "Work, I presume?"

"Always," I answer quickly, piling my plate with french fries and fried chicken tenders. This isn't the type of meal I would normally eat during a lunch recess, but, with the way my stomach is yelling at me to fill it, I couldn't care less. Grabbing a small serving of ranch dressing, I start to chow down without realizing that Izzy and Tom are having a full conversation right next to me.

The vibration of Tom's phone spreads throughout the table and breaks my focus from my food, only for me to notice both Izzy and Tom staring at me in fascination. "What?" I ask, wondering if I had missed something.

"I asked you if you wanted to take a shot at Corporal Alves? You know, see if you can shake him up a little bit. Maybe even get him to crack. Are you up to it?" Tom asks. I can see in his eyes that he's hoping I agree to do this, and for once I feel like we are finally working as a team. As he waits for me to respond, he looks down at his phone to check the time. "Maya, I need to know if you are up to it. We only have a half-hour until we have to go back to court. I know it's a little short notice, but after seeing how you handled Logan, I think you can handle it."

"Yeah, of course. I got this," I assure him, taking one more bite of my food before taking a sip of my soda and wiping my mouth. Throwing my plate away, I wipe my face one more time and mentally prepare myself to take on the Corporal. *Let's do this!*

Chapter 16

After we clean up our mess, all three of us head back into the courtroom and take our seats, each of us more anxious than the last to get this final showdown over with. I'm finally gonna take on the Corporal and see what he has to say for himself.

When Judge Martin enters the room, a small amount of mustard lingering on the collar of his shirt, he calls the court into session. "The Defense can now call their next witness," he instructs, trying to wipe off the lingering condiment without anyone noticing what he is doing.

Showing my respect, I look away while the honorable judge tries to tidy himself up and announce my next witness to testify. "The Defense would like to call Corporal Alves to the stand."

Tired of this dog and pony show, or maybe just afraid that he was about to lose a case to a civilian and a lawyer who had never won a case before, Major Laynard jumps up from his seat. "Objection, Your Honor! The Defense has already had the chance to question this witness. They passed up the chance and, in my opinion, are just wasting the court's time by recalling him!"

There's something about the way that Major Laynard objects this time that makes me realize his bark is worse than his bite.

While I understand why he is objecting, it also feels like he makes a lot of noise in order to shut up the opposing side in hopes of intimidating them so they back down. Unfortunately, for him anyway, I'm not afraid to bite back and I don't get intimidated very easily. Displaying a neutral expression on my face, I explain why I'm recalling the corporal in such simple terms that even a child would understand. "Your Honor, while, yes, the defense had the opportunity to question this witness, my partner and I were still awaiting the analysis of the video evidence from Dr. Fellows. In the light of the new evidence, we would like to recall Corporal Alves to the stand in order to address the questions brought forward by the discovery."

"Very well," Judge Martin responds, lifting his gavel. "Objection overruled." With a loud crack, he seals the deal and motions for me to continue.

A slight rumble makes its way through the courtroom as Corporal Alves passes between the partitions. The way the people sitting on the benches on that side of the room are looking at him speaks volumes. They're filled with disgust, possibly hatred, over the man who would willingly send an innocent young woman to prison for something he had done. I can't say I really blame them, because I too am disgusted by the presence of this man. The only difference is I can't wear my emotions on my sleeve like they can, due to my profession.

The corporal takes his seat in the witness box and is reminded by Judge Martin that he is still under oath. So badly I want to say out loud how it doesn't matter if he's under oath or not, he's already proven himself to be a liar. Instead, I turn around toward my table and take a sip of cold water before I begin.

Tapping the back of my hand to my lips, I remove the excess water and start with my first question but stop before I let a syllable slip from my mouth. "Actually, Your Honor, I apologize.

I mistakenly called Corporal Alves to the stand when he was actually supposed to be called next. My intention was to call a witness from the village by the name of Ms Afri Mullah. But it does not matter this order will work."

The witness was only going to give testimony about the layout of the village but I wanted Alves to believe that I had a witness to the shooting, my words clearly struck a chord with the corporal. The moment he sat down in the witness stand I could tell he was barely hanging on, but with the mere mention of Kandahar and witness, his nerves have gotten the best of him.

Then, a peculiar tremor overtakes his hands, causing them to shake with such intensity that his grasp on reality becomes fragile. In the midst of this unsettling moment, incomprehensible murmurs escape from his lips, creating a disorienting atmosphere in the courtroom. Judge Martin, his countenance etched with worry, directs his gaze toward the troubled individual, his concern palpable.

With genuine concern, Judge Martin persists, repeatedly inquiring about his well-being. Each time the question is posed, Corporal Alves finds himself at the threshold of his composure. Finally, as the third query penetrates the haze surrounding his mind, a dam within him gives way, and an uncontrollable eruption of laughter consumes his being. It is a laughter that defies reason, leaving everyone present transfixed, unable to comprehend the sudden transformation of events.

The room is engulfed in an eerie silence as all eyes remain fixed on Corporal Alves, his hysterical laughter reverberating through the air. The onlookers' curiosity mingles with a deep-rooted bewilderment, unable to grasp the intricate layers that lie beneath the surface of this inexplicable reaction. They find themselves suspended between concern and confusion, their senses held captive by this enigmatic display.

Judge Martin, in a valiant attempt to restore order, exchanges glances with the bailiff, who approaches Corporal Alves cautiously. With a soothing tone, the bailiff seeks to guide him away from the overwhelming grip of laughter, providing a calm presence amidst the bewildering scene. Slowly, the laughter subsides, leaving behind an air of uncertainty and an unspoken question.

Judge Martin announces to the room, "Let's take a ten minute recess, give Corporal Alves time to collect himself."

Taking my seat behind the Defense table, I grab Izzy's hand and give it a much tighter squeeze. We are so close to the finish line and we can all feel it, especially Izzy. She's trying so hard not to smile that I'm pretty sure her face might break if she fights back any longer. I know how she feels because I'm thrilled by how this is going, but I have much more practice at hiding my emotions than my dear friend does.

A woman, who I can only assume is Corporal Alves' wife, rushes over to him as he exits the witness box and walks him out of the room, allowing him to use her much smaller body as means of support. Izzy watches the man who framed her and attempted to use her as a scapegoat, simply shaking her head at the sheer disappointment she is feeling. If she felt anything toward him as I did my commanding officer, she thought of this man as a father figure and this is how he repaid her.

After the ten minute recess is over, the corporal slowly makes his way back into the courtroom and resumes his seat on the witness stand. Judge Martin, still unsure of whether Corporal Alves would be able to continue testifying or not asks: "Are you feeling better now, Corporal?"

Giving a slight nod, Alves blinks hard a few times and answers the judge's question. "Yes, Your Honor. Thank you for asking."

Judge Martin, satisfied with the corporal's answer, looks directly at me. "The Defense may continue questioning the witness."

"Thank you, Your Honor." I respond before walking over to the witness stand, where a still visibly shaken corporal sits in waiting for my next words.

I stood tall, my gaze focused on Corporal Alves, determined to appeal to his sense of honor and integrity. With unwavering conviction, I begin my questioning, my voice filled with respect and admiration.

"Corporal Alves, I have reviewed your remarkable record with great interest. Your unwavering dedication and exemplary service to our country are truly commendable. Today, I implore you to draw upon the strength of your honorable military background and speak the truth."

A palpable tension filled the courtroom as the attorney delved into the marine's distinguished achievements. I meticulously highlight his numerous commendations, medals, and accolades, symbols of his outstanding character and commitment to upholding the highest standards of the military.

"Corporal Alves, your military career has been a testament to your integrity, your adherence to the values that make our armed forces strong. You have proven yourself time and again, demonstrating unwavering courage, loyalty, and dedication to your fellow marines and the mission at hand."

Pausing for a moment, allowed the weight of Corporal Alves' impeccable military record to settle in the room. I continued, my voice filled with a mix of admiration and urgency.

"In light of your distinguished service, I ask you to reflect on the core principles that guided you throughout your military journey. Honor, integrity, and loyalty are not just words; they are the bedrock of your character. I implore you, Corporal Alves, to summon the strength of your convictions and speak the truth here today."

With each word, I seek to appeal to the marine's deep-seated sense of honor, calling upon his integrity to rise above any temptation to deceive. I remind him of the trust placed in him by his comrades and the responsibility that came with bearing the title of a Marine.

"Corporal Alves, the truth is not only a testament to your character but also a solemn duty to justice. Your comrades, your unit, and the values you hold dear are counting on you to uphold the integrity that has defined your military career."

As I conclude my impassioned appeal, a hushed silence enveloped the courtroom. All eyes remained fixed on Corporal Alves, awaiting his response. The weight of his own honor and the attorney's plea hung in the air, urging him to shed the web of deceit and reveal the truth, for it was within that truth that his true strength as a Marine lay.

My words have struck a chord, seeking to break through the barriers of deception and falsehood. It was a plea infused with the genuine belief in the marine's capacity to rise above, to find solace and redemption in the path of truth.

As the courtroom held its collective breath, all hopes rested on Corporal Alves, his honorable military record and his sense of duty serving as beacons of inspiration.

Major Laynard gets to his feet " Your Honor any chance possibly we might get a question in the near future from the defence?"

Judge Martin " I agree. We are all aware of Corporal Alves' impeccable and distinguished record. Please ask a question, Ms. Hartwell."

Tom is sitting at the defence table. He is transfixed, beguiled and full of admiration for my oratory skills and the way the whole panel is hanging on every syllable of what I have uttered. I am setting this up perfectly.

I move back towards Tom so the panel of members have a clear view of Corporal Alves. Now I can change my tact.

"Corporal Alves, why do you think my client would shoot all of those people?"

"Be—because she believed they were responsible for the death of her boyfriend. She wanted revenge," he explains, trying to stick to his previous story.

"But didn't the defendant break up with her boyfriend, Second Lieutenant Miguel Gomez, a month before he was killed? They weren't on speaking terms by the time he left for his mission. So, why would she want to exact revenge for someone she wasn't speaking to?" I ask, driving home the fact that his previous statement and testimony were based on a lie.

"I—I don't know. I didn't even know they had broken up," he admits, stumbling over himself. "Just b—because they weren't t—talk... talking doesn't mean that she wasn't grieving over his death."

"True, but how do you explain your name being the original name on the M16A2's rifle cam? How did your name get deleted, unsuccessfully I might add, and replaced with Second Lieutenant Isabella Martinez-Garcia's? We all heard what Dr. Fellows said, the meta data of the video footage had been tampered with. So how did your name get swapped with hers?" I ask, ready to pounce at the just the right second and rip his throat out like a lion on the hunt.

"Again, I don't know. I'm not good with computers. It took both my daughter and wife three days to teach me how to check the email on my cell phone. I have no clue how any of that technological stuff works," he explains, foolishly leaving an opening for me.

"But you do admit that the video recording belongs to you and that you are the Marine pulling the trigger?" I ask, slowly reeling him in. I'm just waiting for my moment, where I can yank him out of his comfort zone, gut him, and hang him on my wall like a trophy. He's my target and I'm aiming all missiles his way right now, and I know that he can see it coming as well.

"No! I didn't admit to any of that!" he wails, trying to persuade me to back off a little bit.

"You didn't deny any of it either! You were the one who took the lives of those three civilians, weren't you, Corporal Alves?" The intensity in my voice grew with each word, as I confronted the marine head-on. The weight of the accusation hung heavily in the air, demanding a response, a confession.

Before Corporal Alves could reply, Major Laynard's objection rudely interrupted the proceedings. "Objection! Ms. Hartwell is badgering the witness, Your Honor," he yelled, attempting to salvage his crumbling case.

Judge Martin, who had been carefully observing the situation, cocked his head to the side, considering the objection. In an unexpected turn, he responded, acknowledging the attorney's authority over her witness. "It's her witness, Major." The judge's response indicated his willingness to allow me to continue my line of questioning.

Turning back towards me, Judge Martin waved me on, granting permission to proceed. "Please proceed, Ms. Hartwell," he said, his tone encouraging and attentive.

"Thank you, Your Honor," I acknowledged, appreciating the judge's recognition of the importance of the moment. Sensing the tide shifting, I swiftly requested permission to treat the witness as hostile, recognizing the need to push the boundaries of traditional questioning. I knew the path this back-and-forth was leading us towards.

"Permission to treat the witness as hostile?" I asked, my voice unwavering, already anticipating the response that lay ahead.

"Permission granted," Judge Martin quickly responded, his own excitement apparent as he was drawn into the unfolding drama.

With newfound authorization, I locked eyes with Corporal Alves, determination burning within me. Leaning forward, my hands tightly gripping the banister, I pressed forward, my voice firm and unyielding. "Corporal Alves, were you or were you not the person responsible for the death of those three civilians? I remind you that you are under oath!"

A flicker of confusion crossed Corporal Alves' face, his eyes betraying his internal struggle. The pressure mounted, and his resolve began to crumble. "Yes. I mean, no. I mean, God, I don't know. You have me all confused!" he yelled, his voice reflecting his desperation.

Seizing the moment, I refused to relent. "Admit it, Corporal! You killed those three people and framed an innocent woman! Didn't you?!" I demanded, finally ready to capture the prey I had been meticulously playing with.

And just like that, Corporal Alves cracked wide open, his confession tumbling out. "Yes, okay?! I did it! You don't understand, do you? I couldn't stand idly by while those people got away with the murder of my comrades. Every night, their screams for help haunted my dreams. The first night of peace I had was after I shot those people. I don't care if the three who died weren't responsible for the Marines' deaths. It was only a matter of time before their bombs claimed more innocent lives!"

Corporal Alves' admission left me stunned. The depth of his reasoning was beyond what I had anticipated. Suppressing the lump in my throat, I composed myself and turned towards Judge Martin, ready to seize this pivotal moment.

"Your Honor, as you can see, this trial and the treatment my client has endured are a complete miscarriage of justice," I declared, my voice steady but filled with conviction. "If it weren't for Corporal Alves and those who colluded with him in this elaborate fabrication, my client would be living a carefree life, and this trial would never have come to pass. I motion for the charges against my client to be dismissed.

Judge Martin's eyes flicker around, taking in the view of the room. He stays silent for a moment, leaving me standing in front of him as I question what I should do next. Finally, he speaks, slowly and concisely, making sure that everyone in the room understands what he is about to say. "Ms. Hartwell, please take your seat." Doing as he says, I sit down next to Izzy and keep my eyes glued on him as I wait for his decision. "Although I agree with every word you said, Ms. Hartwell, I don't have the power to bring each and every person who was in on this coup to justice. However, I do believe that the way Second Lieutenant Isabella Martinez-Garcia has been treated during her imprisonment and subsequent trial is disturbing. Witnesses, who were under oath, had the gall to sit on the witness stand and lie about their fellow Marine, knowing she was not responsible for the death of three innocent civilians. Having served my time in the Marines, this entire case has been a disappointment. Brothers in arms have turned on their sister, and that is not what the Marines stand for. How can we, as soldiers, be heroes in the eyes of young children if we are throwing one another under the bus? It's sickening. With that being said, I hereby order the immediate release of Second Lieutenant Isabella Martinez-Garcia and dismiss all charges pertaining to this case."

For the first time since this trial began, the sound of the gavel smashing down on the judge's bench sounds as beautiful as a symphony. Izzy grabs my arm and springs up from her chair, bringing me with her. Throwing her arms around my neck, this time not squeezing nearly as tightly, and jumping for joy, she repeats the words, "You did it, Maya! You did it! I'm free."

I join her for a moment, hopping up and down in glee, only to stop when I notice Judge Martin speaking to the bailiff and pointing towards the back of the room. Izzy follows my eyes, and together we watch as the bailiff walks in the direction the judge was pointing and approaches Corporal Alves, Staff Sergeant Morgan Wellbeck and First Lieutenant Dan Thomas. We look on as he arrests them and marches them off to the brig.

Izzy slips her hand into mine and we watch as the corporal puts up a small struggle before he is handcuffed and taken out of the courtroom. I had done it—*we* had done it. Izzy is now free and the real killer will be behind bars within a matter of minutes.

Chapter 17

Rushing back to my hotel room, I quickly change my clothes and throw all of my belongings, which are strewn around the room, into my luggage. I'm supposed to leave tomorrow morning, but with Izzy finally home, I promised her that I would spend my last night at her place. Looking in the bathroom mirror before I head out to meet my friend, Tom, and Logan at a nearby bar, I make sure the jeans I threw on make me look as good as I feel right now. *Damn, I do look hot tonight!*

Satisfied with my final look, I throw on some flats, grab my luggage, and close the door behind me. As I approach the front desk, I slide the older woman at the computer my room key and inform her that I will be checking out early.

The woman furrows her brow and looks around the lobby, seemingly confused. "Will your husband be dropping off the extra room key? If not, I will have to charge you a $20 deactivation fee."

"What husband? You must have me confused with another guest, ma'am. I'm not married," I correct her, sure that she must think I'm half of another couple who has been staying here.

"No, I'm not confusing you with anyone else. Room 117. Your husband arrived shortly after you checked in and said you had forgotten to grab an extra key for him. I only know this because I was the one who activated the swipe card for him and warned him about the fee if the extra key wasn't returned at check out." She is so sure of herself as she tells me this story that I know she must be telling the truth—or she's a crazy old bat trying to hustle me out of 20 bucks. Either way, this incident confirms my suspicions that my supposed 'husband' has been entering my room and tampering with my belongings. Most likely the culprit is someone from the Marines. Who else could it be? Now I need to decided whether I should review the footage, file a complaint, and consider the time and potential outcome. In a split second I make my decision: Izzy is innocent and cleared and I should prioritise my other case, so I let it go.

"Just charge the fee to my card, please. I really have to get going." I slide her my credit card, sign the slip to agree to the charges, and head out the door to my car. Throwing my luggage into my trunk, I hop in the driver's seat and let out a deep breath as I prepare myself to let loose, possibly even have some fun. It's been a hell of a week and I know that as soon as I get back to San Francisco I'm going to be buried in case prep work. I might as well enjoy my last day here before I have to get back to my real life.

Pulling out of the parking lot, I hang a left and drive three more blocks until I reach the bar. Shutting off the engine, I get out of my car and take a good look at the so-called best saloon in town. *Saloon? Where am I, the wild west?* With the old stained-glass windows and the sound of honky tonk music clinging to the night air, this isn't the type of bar I would normally frequent. However, it's Izzy's favorite place to grab a beer so what kind of friend would I be if I told her no?

As soon as I push open the door and step inside, I spot Izzy in the back corner, leaning against the jukebox. My eyes scan the room, looking for the other half of our party of four. At the end of the bar I see Tom and Logan alternating between shots of, what appears to be, tequila and mugs of foamy beer.

Logan notices me standing at the door first and rushes over to Izzy, pointing me out. A big smile spreads across her face, only broken when she turns around and punches a few buttons on the gigantic, ancient machine. When she turns back around, an evil smirk is on her lips and I know she's up to something.

Izzy makes her way over to me just as Pink Floyd's "Another Brick in the Wall" begins to play. She gives me a hug when I'm finally within reach, her breath smelling of scotch and stale cigarettes. "I played this song for you because I know it's your favorite," she half whispers, half yells in my ear.

"Thank you," I yell back as the sound of the guitar starts to take over the room. "I see you started drinking without me."

"Yeah, sorry. I saved you a shot, though," she informs me, pointing at the empty bar. "Well, I thought I did anyway." Her speech is slurred already, which means it's either going to be a very interesting night or I'm going to be holding her hair back as she pukes in the toilet. "You w—want a b—beer?" she asks, hiccups breaking up her words.

"Sure, I'll take a beer. But only if you drink a glass of water. Deal?" Agreeing with my bargain, Izzy orders me a tall, near-ly-cold mug of beer and one ice water. Sitting with her at the bar, I feel a strange sense of calm coming over me. This is the first time I've actually allowed myself to relax in who knows how long, and I'm kind of enjoying it–maybe a little too much.

Izzy gulps down her glass of water and drinks another one before she orders all four of us a round of shots. Throwing mine back, and trying not to choke from the harsh burn as the liquid rushes down my throat, I do myself a favor and cut myself off for the rest of the night. While the other three continue taking shots, I order myself a Cherry Coke and chew on the stem of the maraschino cherry the bartender was nice enough to add in my drink.

As we sit there, enjoying our time together and singing along to oldies on the jukebox, I feel my phone vibrating in my pants pocket. Sliding it out of its denim holster, I swipe the screen to bring the device back to life and spot a familiar anonymous sender's email in my notifications. Figuring the new message is about the ransom demand he had mentioned earlier, I open the message out of curiosity to see if my presumption is correct. However, this message is different from the others. It has nothing to do with my father, and the only thing the message says is: *You look nice in those jeans. You should wear them more often.*

My heart begins to race as I look around the room, hoping to find someone on their phone and acting suspiciously. For the first time in my entire life since the smartphone has been invented, absolutely no one is on their phone. Suddenly, my phone rings, causing me to nearly jump out of my skin. Bringing my attention to the screen, I answer the call as soon as I see Wren's name flash across the caller ID.

"Hello? Wren?" I ask, trying to slow my breathing down as I keep on the room, looking out for whoever may be watching me.

"Maya, are you okay?" he asks, his voice overflowing with concern.

"Yeah, I think so." Facing forward toward the rest of the bar, I walk backward until I reach the women's bathroom. I use the heel of my shoe to open the door and step inside. "Wren, whoever has been emailing me is in this bar with me."

"I know, that's why I'm calling you. I managed to get through the firewall and pinpoint Concerned Citizen's location. Then,

I saw that you had received a new email and that the person was in the same location as you are right now. I just wanted to make sure that you are okay." Although I'm happy that Wren is a good enough friend to check up on me and make sure I'm alright, I'm more interested in finding out who this creep is. "Maya, are you there? What do you want me to do?"

That's when it hits me. I know exactly what to do. If no one is on their phone when I'm watching, then I will blow up their phone so much that they are forced to look at their phone. That is when I'll catch them in the act. "Hey, Wren, I want you to spam their email continuously. Do it until I tell you to stop."

"You're the boss!"

Chapter 18

"Starting now," Wren announces as I exit the women's bathroom, my eyes scanning the room from wall to wall. I look for anyone who is on their phone, which apparently has changed since I went into the lady's room because now everyone is staring at their screen. "Do you see them yet?"

"No, everyone is on their phones. It's hard to figure out who it is unless I start peeking over people's shoulders. I'm at a bar on a Marine base, people don't take too kindly to that," I whisper, ducking behind a much taller man when I notice Izzy looking for me. With her being drunk, there's no way I'm going to be able to figure out who has been trying to extort me while she's loudly following behind.

"Oh, really? It's about time you tell me why you are really in San Diego," Wren teases.

"Yeah, like you didn't know this entire time. You're still spamming that inbox right?" I confirm, ensuring that I'm not making a fool out of myself, moving from side to side and peeking over shoulders for nothing.

Wren lets out a deep sigh and mumbles something under his breath. "Yes, Maya. The email count is about to hit three-hundred, so his phone should be blowing up. Constant notifications, making it really hard to ignore. If this keeps going any longer, it's going to freeze up his phone and he won't be able to do anything on it. So you might want to look for someone who looks frustrated because their phone isn't working."

"Oh! That's a good idea." Still scanning the room, I notice one person in particular poking at their screen in the dark corner of the bar. "Wren, I'm going to have you stop spamming for a second. I'll tell you when to start again." For the next five minutes, while still managing to maintain a distance between myself and Izzy, I watch as the bar patrons meet up with friends or start conversing, putting their phones down one by one. "Alright, start it again."

With a watchful eye on the person in the corner of the bar, I move toward the back wall and follow them toward the hallway. Closing the distance between us, the consistent tapping on their phone screen sounds a lot like pure frustration. Hiding my phone behind my back, I step to their left and stop directly in front of them, giving off a look of concern. "Everything okay, Tom? Something wrong with your phone?"

"Oh, no." he chuckles, glancing up for a split second. "I'm just wrapping up the last bit of the case files. You know, crossing my T's, dotting the I's. All that mumbo jumbo. You're a lawyer, you know how it is."

"Yeah I do." I laugh, mimicking his. "You know what, I'm gonna go get a drink. Would you like one?"

"Sure. Just a draft please. I'll be there in a minute," he says, a nervous smile attempting to break up his sincere one. "Thanks!"

Giving him an assuring nod, I hold back when someone steps in front of me, using the person's large body as a human camouflage. Placing the phone against my ear, I whisper to Wren to pause for a second again and watch as Tom slides his phone in his pocket. Allowing the possible culprit's phone to rest for a minute, my attention stays on him as he walks toward the bar, only for me to tell Wren to start spamming again.

Sure enough, as soon as Wren tells me he has started, Tom pulls his phone back out of his pocket and begins to tap on the screen aggressively. "I got him, Wren. I'll call you back." I inform my helpful spy friend before hanging up. Marching up to Tom, I feel my hands ball up into fists but force my body to release the hold. I don't want to hit the guy physically, just where it hurts—his ego. Tom's eyes shift up as I approach him, a flash of fear smothered in some type of strange adoration in them as he looks me up and down. "Hey, Tom. Still tying up loose ends or are you sending me another weird email about my dead father?" I ask him, my words practically coming out as a hiss.

"W—what are you talking about, Maya?" he laughs, looking behind him as he backs up and tries to get away from me.

Refusing to let him off that easy, I keep walking forward, pushing him closer to the front of the bar. Eventually he will run into a wall and won't be able to escape from my question. "Rule number one of being a good lawyer, Tom; never ask a question you don't already know the answer to. Why were you sending me those emails about my father, Tom? I know it was you, so you might as well just admit it."

Taking one more step back, he finally reaches the wall and can't move back any further. By now everyone in the bar is staring at us, including Izzy and an inebriated Logan. No one in the room makes a move as they try to figure out what the hell is going on. Tom tries to step to the side to get around me, but Izzy jumps in front of him. Even though she has no clue why I'm confronting her lawyer, she's still my girl and has my back. Plus, she knows I have my reasons.

"Look, Tom. I don't know what you did to my... my friend, but you better do what she says or I'll kick your ass. I've already been to prison, so it's no difference to me if I spend another night in a jail cell," Izzy threatens him, her words slurred and running together.

Throwing his hands in the air as if we are holding him at gunpoint, Tom surrenders and starts to expose the truth behind his actions. "Fine! I admit that I sent those emails. But, in my defense, I only did it to distract you from defending Izzy and that's only because I was ordered to by a superior officer. The military had hacked your emails, saw the original email from the Concerned Citizen guy and decided to double down on it by sending numerous emails to try and distract you from the case. I was told not to tell you or let you win the case at any costs and, honestly, I didn't want an ex-Marine to take my thunder. But toward the end of the case, I started to feel guilty about what I had done. I started to appreciate you for your abilities in the courtroom, which is why I let you question those witnesses in the end. I was the reason we won."

"Well, it looks like more people are reading my emails than the Washington Post lately. But, Tom, let me let you in on a little secret. The reason you have never and will never win a case is because you are a spineless worm. You're a doormat, which means you are never going to get ahead. I hope you enjoyed the feeling of winning a case, because I guarantee you that it's the only time you will experience it." Grabbing Izzy by the hand, I lead her out of the bar and walk over to my car. "Look, Izzy, I know I was supposed to stay the night with you tonight but–" I start to explain before she cuts me off.

"Get out of here! You have a trial to prepare for and you have already been here much longer than you originally planned. Don't worry about me, I already called an Uber to take me home." Izzy holds out her arms and embraces me in one more hug, squeezing tightly before she says one more thing. "Thank you so much, Maya. You saved my life, seriously. I owe you."

Unwinding my arms from around her body, I hold onto her hand for a few more seconds. "You don't owe me, Izzy. Just come visit me every once in a while and we'll call it even, okay?"

The big beautiful smile that I had been looking forward to seeing since I first arrived spreads across her face, and I can already tell I'm going to miss it as soon as I leave. "Sounds fair to me. Drive safe!"

Hopping into the driver's seat, I start my car and wave out the window as I head back home; a trail of dust behind me, covering up the lies I had exposed at the San Diego Marine Base.

Chapter 19

Nothing feels sweeter than pulling into the driveway of my home, especially now that I have another win under my belt. The entire drive I spent thinking about every aspect of the case, from how many layers of deceit I had to uncover to the end result. While I'm super happy that Izzy's name is cleared and the case is dismissed, I can't help but still feel deeply annoyed by Tom's actions. *I mean, seriously, who does that?*

The strange part is, even if Tom's emails were merely speculation and he was willing to deal out a low blow in order to distract me, his claims might have had a kernel of truth in there. If he hadn't emailed me, I would have never had Wren start digging into the case files which means I would have never known about the death threats my father was receiving. Still, even if Tom's strange messages were purely speculation, I oddly find myself interested in looking into my father's death and discovering the truth–even if it's to put my worries at ease.

However, I know if I want to keep digging, I'm going to need a partner and there is no one else I can think of other than Wren. *Would he even be interested though?* Putting myself out there–just like I had when I confronted Tom–while also wanting to clear my mind, I redial Wren's phone number.

Picking up on the first ring, he answers the call with a question, "Don't you ever get tired of talking to me? I just got off the phone with you like eight hours ago."

Letting out a soft laugh, I respond with a sarcastic remark. "Guess I just missed your annoying ass sense of humor." With the phone cushioned between the side of my head and my shoulder, I unlock my front door and toss my car keys on the table. "Anyway, I was just calling to see if you would be willing to come down to San Francisco and help me delve into my father's case."

"Yeah, of course!" he agrees without hesitation. "I'm actually about to catch a flight right now. Why don't I give you a call when I get home and we'll set up a time for me to fly out there?"

"Sounds great. Thank you! I will talk to you then. Bye!" I listen to him say goodbye before hanging up and feel the strange sensation of a smile spreading across my lips. *Why am I smiling? What does that mean? Could I possibly have feelings for Wren? Is that even possible?*

Not wanting to dwell on my possible feelings for a good friend for too long, I drink a couple glasses of wine before turning on some anime to watch for escapism. Soon after, though, I feel my eyelids beginning to close and give into temptation as I fall asleep on the couch.

Epilogue

I wake up to loud knocking at my front door. Slowly, I move through the house, still a little bleary eyed and a tiny bit hungover from last night's wine. Cracking the door open, I take a peek around the door and find Wren standing on my front porch.

"Wren? What are you doing here?" I ask, trying my best not to let a yawn interrupt my question.

"I told you I was catching a flight, I just didn't say where." Shaking my head in disbelief, I open the door the rest of the way and let him into the house. Moving his head from side to side, he looks over my humble abode and nods in approval. "Nice place."

"Thanks," I tell him as I walk toward my bedroom and grab my robe, eager to cover up the baggy pair of sweatpants and Marine's T-shirt I dozed off in last night. "How's Landsfield Ridge?" I ask him as he takes a seat on the couch and opens his luggage.

I make my way to the kitchen to fix us both a cup of coffee and wait for his response.

"It's good," he calls out to me. "Kinda boring now that you left though. That girl you helped and her family are doing pretty good too. Word around town is that she is looking into some state colleges. I imagine she wants to get as far away from town as possible after what happened, and I can't really blame her."

"Yeah, I can't either." I yell out to him, adding a spoonful of sugar and some cream to each cup. By the time I get back to the living room, he has a small office setup, complete with a laptop, router, and wireless printer. On the floor lies a thick stack of files, nearly as high as the coffee table they are stacked against. "What's all this?" I ask, struggling to figure out if this is reality or I'm having some lucid dream I can't get out of.

Wren stands up from the couch and grabs my hand in a comforting manner. "I kind of lied when I told you that I couldn't find anything about your father's death. I actually found a lot, but I didn't want to tell you over the phone. You never know who's listening, you know?"

"Okay," I tell him, as I start to lean more toward this all being a lucid dream. Slowly sinking down to the floor, I begin to look through the files he brought with him. "How did you get all this stuff, Wren? I mean, like, how did you get so good at computer hacking?"

"You wouldn't want to know, Maya but hopefully one day I can tell you."

Letting out a nervous laugh, I take a sip of my coffee and hope the caffeine begins to kick in if I'm going to be expected to keep up with Wren's jokes. Wiping the remaining coffee off my lips, I open the first file on top of the stack and start reading. "I guess we should get to work then, huh?"

"Yep, I guess so." Wren smiles, his eyes going back to his computer screen.

The feeling of Wren and I working together is a satisfying level of comfort, even though we are just sitting here quietly and focusing on our own tasks. Although I'm trying to read over the documents in front of me, I can't help but wonder if it will always be like this when I'm with him—and part of me is hoping I might get the chance to find out.

My phone buzzes beside me, a new email notification flashing across the screen. Opening the email, I notice the name I thought I had left behind in San Diego.

Long time, no talk, Ms. Hartwell.

If you want to know the truth about your father, then you're going to need more than a computer hacker to find me. Respond to my emails, follow my instructions, and the truth will be yours.

Concerned Citizen

Echoes of Betrayal (Quest for Justice) Series Book 3 is now available on Amazon

Heads Up! – Here is the back cover blurb to **Echoes of Betrayal (Quest for Justice) Series Book 3** in the series, released **October 2023**

Maya Hartwell once again finds herself in the courtroom, confronting a case that will push her limits in ways she could never have foreseen. This time, her unwavering mission is to take down Christopher McLaughlin, a ruthless hitman responsible for her father's murder. Standing by her side, her librarian friend Wren with his unfathomable skills remains a steadfast source of support and assistance.

Armed with unorthodox evidence, Maya navigates a maze of legal obstacles, all the while facing mounting pressure from a mob determined to set McLaughlin free and grappling with a shocking betrayal from someone she once considered a safe confidant.

This thrilling tale of lies and truth, revenge and justice, and the fine line between friends and enemies is the third book of the Maya Hartwell Quest for Justice series—and is guaranteed to keep you guessing until the very end.

Up Next for Maya Hartwell

Echoes of the Past (Quest for Justice) Series Book – Published on Amazon. **https://books2read.com/u/baq9O2**
Room of Echoes (Quest for Justice) Series Book 2 – Published on Amazon **https://books2read.com/u/m0WqvA**
Echoes of Betrayal (Quest for Justice) Series Book 3 - Published on Amazon **https://books2read.com/u/mZq97B**
Book 4 in the Quest for Justice Series Coming Q2 2024 or sooner!

Newsletter Sign Up

You can find out more about my books and any up coming news at my website via this link **www.gabbyblack.com** or indeed just sign up for my newsletter by going to the website.

About the Author

Get ready to embark on an exciting journey into the captivating world of mystery, courtroom drama, crime, and investigation with Gabby Black's thrilling novels. As an ardent enthusiast of these genres, I pour my heart and soul into weaving stories that will keep you eagerly turning the pages, filled with suspense, unexpected plot twists, and enigmatic mysteries that will keep you guessing until the very last word.

With a background spanning nine years in the Justice System, I draw upon both my vivid imagination and real-life experiences to craft gripping tales that will leave you absolutely spellbound. When I'm not immersed in writing, I'm out there exploring the world through travel, connecting with diverse people, seeking out new adventures, and drawing inspiration for my next novel.

Oh, and did I mention I'm a lover of fine wine, well lets be honest its actually most wine! You might have picked up on that from the pages of my books.

So, won't you join me on this exhilarating journey into the un-known, where every page holds the promise of discovery and excitement? Grab one of my novels and let's dive into a world where thrilling stories await, and unforgettable adventures are just a page turn away. Cheers to the mysteries that lie ahead!

Thank you so much for reading and I sincerely hope you enjoyed the third book in the new 'Quest for Justice' series. As an independent author, I am incredibly grateful for your support. I would love if you could take just a few moments to write a review. Your reviews are immensely helpful and I do genuinely read each and every single one. For those of you who are reading from an ipad, phone or pc here is a direct link to leave a review **https://rebrand.ly/1d6iumz** otherwise kindly log into your Amazon account, find the book and leave a review. I truly appreciate your time and feedback. Thanks Immensely!

You can find out more about me and my books at my website via this link **www.gabbyblack.com**

Printed in Great Britain
by Amazon

42182651R00096